英文檢定考、升學考、關鍵文法要點！
全書10堂英文課，一次掌握！

使用說明

☆ **一、本課學習要點**

　　全書共分為10課，包含各種被英文學習者當作是挑戰、甚至是瓶頸的文法，在每課開始學習前，先看「本課學習要點」，複習一下你可能以前聽過的規則，了解接下來要學習的重點。

☆ **二、例句說明**

　　在例句中說明每個文法演變的步驟，清楚呈現每個句子元素代表的意義。

☆ **三、重點筆記**

　　有規則就會有例外，「重點筆記」整理出一些比較容易被忽略的文法要點，幫助你全面掌握每課中呈現的句型！

☆ **四、文法總複習**

　　每課中，講解完一個文法規則，就會附註「文法練習站」，而每課學習完之後，就會有「文法總複習」。別怕面對挑戰！每答對一個題目，就是你更上一層樓的證明。過完這些關卡，就能修煉成為文法高手！

Preface

　　許多英語學習者，看到比較長的句子，或者像是倒裝句、複合句等特殊的句型，就會望而卻步，覺得自己看不懂、甚至想放棄。其實，當遇到很長的句子、或是較為複雜的句型，只要掌握兩個原則：

> ❶ 找出最主要主詞和動詞。
> ❷ 把句子分段。

例如：

I'm not on any social network, but my children and people of their age feel like they know each other before they meet because they're connected online.

　　這句話看起來很長，可是找到5組主詞加動詞：

❶ I'm not on any social network,

❷ but my children and of people their age feel like

❸ they know each other

❹ before they meet

❺ because they're connected online

　　在上面五組主詞加動詞中，❶是屬於主要子句，它不是任何動作的受詞、也沒有接在從屬連接詞之後。每個小段的意思都看懂之後，再慢慢把意思拼湊起來，就可以了解這句話的意思：

　　「我沒有加入任何社群網站，但是我的小孩、以及他們的同儕，在彼此見面之前，就覺得他們已經認識彼此，因為他們有在線上連結。」

學文法不只是背規則

　　由上述的例子可知，學文法不只是要背很多公式、破解很多刁鑽的考題；最終的目的是，我們要能夠正確地分析句子。目的在於，在閱讀時，就算是長兩、三行的句子，也能看懂；在寫作時，能夠寫出合文法邏輯的句子，朝著成為文法高手的終極目標邁進！

　　本書在講解文法時，著重在解析一個長句、或者一個複雜的句子，是怎麼演變成為現在的樣子？就像學習形容詞子句時，最開始時常都是由合併句子開始的，像是： a I like the girl. 和 b The girl is wearing a pink dress. 兩句合併成 I like the girl who is wearing a pink dress. （我喜歡穿粉紅色洋裝的那個女生。）

　　但是，為什麼一定要合併？為什麼一定要加形容詞子句呢？因為沒有加上後面那一段的話，聽話的人不知道說話的人在講的是哪一個女生。很多文法要使用時，都是有它的意義存在。這本書目的，不只是講解文法規則，更希望清楚呈現，文法使用的時機、還有它代表的意思。因此，從例句中學習文法，是必要的！

圖表式學習

　　為了清楚表示文法的規則與其中的意義，本書使用了大量的圖表來呈現例句，並且在例句旁，有附註清楚的說明，在閱讀這些說明的過程中，可以更了解形容詞子句、倒裝句、以及連接詞等等的文法規則，是如何衍生而來，每個句子的元素，又各自扮演了什麼角色。條列式的說明及可愛的插畫，讓你在頭上冒問號之前，就不小心看懂了！

Contents

使用説明 ／002　　前言 ／003

Lesson 1

「如果我有100萬，就太棒了！」

If I had a million dollars, that would be wonderful!

假設語氣與常用句型

📄 **條件式假設** ／012
　❶ 單純描述條件的假設 ／012
　❷ 與現在事實相反的假設 ／014
　❸ 與過去事實相反的假設 ／017
　❹ 與未來情況相反的假設 ／019

📄 **願望式假設** ／022
　❶ 與現在事實不符的假設願望 ／022
　❷ 與過去事實不符的假設願望 ／023

Lesson 1【文法總複習】／026

Lesson 2

「那個戴眼鏡的女孩，是我的菜！」

The girl who wears glasses is my type.

關係代名詞與子句 I

📄 **關係代名詞** ／030
　❶ 限定關係子句 ／031
　❷ 非限定關係子句 ／049

Lesson 2【文法總複習】／054

「轉角的那間咖啡店，是我和她相遇的地方。」
The café at the corner is the place I first met her.

關係代名詞與子句 II

📑 **有介系詞的關係子句** /058
　❶ 限定關係子句 /058
　❷ 非限定關係子句 /060

📑 **關係副詞引導關係子句** /064
　❶ where 代表「地方」 /064
　❷ when 代表「時間」 /067
　❸ why代表「原因」 /070
　❹ how代表「方式」 /072
　❺ 關係副詞的省略 /075

📑 **複合關係代名詞** /077
　❶ whoever指「無論誰」 /077
　❷ whomever 指「無論誰」（受格） /078
　❸ whosever 指「無論誰的」 /079
　❹ whatever 指「無論什麼；無論何事」 /079
　❺ whichever 指「無論哪一個」 /081
　❻ wherever指「無論何處」 /082

Lesson 3【文法總複習】 /085

「那就是命運的安排，不是嗎？」
This is destiny, isn't it?

疑問句構

📑 **一般疑問句** /088
　❶ 助動詞疑問句 /088
　❷ 疑問詞疑問句 /090

📋 **附加問句** ／095
　❶ 一般直述句的附加問句 ／096
　❷ 特殊主詞的附加問句 ／098
　❸ 祈使句的附加問句 ／100

📋 **間接問句** ／102
　❶ 助動詞（含be動詞）疑問句 ／102
　❷ 疑問詞疑問句 ／104

Lesson 4 【**文法總複習**】 ／111

「就是她，我一眼就看到的人。」
It is her that I fell in love with at the first sight.

強調語氣 I ──分裂句

📋 **It-分裂句** ／116
　❶ 強調主詞 ／118
　❷ 強調受詞 ／118
　❸ 強調副詞 ／119

📋 **Wh-分裂句** ／125

Lesson 5 【**文法總複習**】 ／130

「若沒遇見她，我人生就是黑白的！」
Had I not met her, I would be tired of my life!

強調語氣 I ──倒裝句構

📋 **否定倒裝句構** ／134
　❶ be動詞的否定倒裝 ／134
　❷ 助動詞的否定倒裝 ／136
　❸ 一般動詞的否定倒裝 ／138

📑 **only倒裝句構** ╱139

📑 **so/such倒裝句構** ╱145
  ❶ so ... that ... 倒裝 ╱145
  ❷ such ... that ... 倒裝 ╱148

📑 **地方副詞倒裝句構** ╱151
  ❶ 動詞為be動詞的倒裝 ╱151
  ❷ 動詞為不及物動詞的倒裝 ╱151
  ❸ be動詞＋分詞的倒裝 ╱154

📑 **假設倒裝句構** ╱156
  ❶ 與現在事實相反的假設倒裝句 ╱157
  ❷ 與過去事實相反的假設倒裝句 ╱158
  ❸ 表示未來「萬一」的假設倒裝句 ╱159

Lesson 6【文法總複習】 ╱162

Lesson 7

「我那麼喜歡她，她卻不看我一眼！」
Much as I like her, she keeps ignoring me.

強調語氣Ⅲ—— 比較級與讓步子句

📑 **比較級的強調** ╱166
  ❶ 受詞移位 ╱166
  ❷ 形容詞移位 ╱169
  ❸ 副詞移位 ╱171

📑 **讓步子句的強調** ╱174
  ❶ 名詞移位 ╱175
  ❷ 形容詞移位 ╱177
  ❸ 副詞移位 ╱179
  ❹ 動詞移位 ╱183

Lesson 7【文法總複習】 ╱186

「看著她，我感覺心跳加快。」

Looking at her, I feel my heart is racing.

分詞構句

📋 什麼時候可以用分詞構句 ／190

📋 要將哪一個句子簡化？ ／190

📋 形成分詞構句的方式 ／192

❶ 主動句 ／194
❷ 被動句 ／196
❸ 否定句 ／199
❹ 完成式 ／202
❺ 被動完成式 ／204
❻ 不省略連接詞的分詞構句 ／207

📋 獨立分詞構句 ／210
❶ 不省略主詞 ／210
❷ 可省略主詞 ／213

Lesson 8【文法總複習】／219

「然而，卻得不到結果。」

However, I can't see our future.

轉承語

📋 表達立場或意見 ／222

📋 逐點列述 ／224

📋 提出例證 ／227

📋 表達時間順序 ／229

📋 開啟話題或轉換話題 ／231

📋 **加強語氣** ／233

📋 **表達對比** ／235

📋 **表示轉折或讓步** ／237

📋 **表示原因或結果** ／239

📋 **提出解釋或補充說明** ／241

📋 **表達結論** ／242

Lesson 9【**文法總複習**】／244

Lesson 10

「每當我思念她，我就讀英文詩。」

Whenever I miss her, I read English poetry.

複合句構

📋 **區分四種英文句型結構** ／248

❶ 單句 ／248

❷ 合句 ／250

❸ 複句 ／251

❹ 複合句 ／252

Lesson 10【**文法總複習**】／254

Lesson 1

假設語氣與
常用句型

「如果我有100萬，就太棒了！」

If I had a million dollars, that would be wonderful!

假設語氣與常用句型

　　假設語氣是用來表達假設的句型。英文的假設語氣涉及「事實」，有些假設的條件是有可能發生的，只要條件成立，假設就成立；有些假設的條件則是「純想像」的，這類假設往往與事實相反。要正確使用假設語氣，必須要有一定的邏輯觀念，才能以正確的時態來表達假設語氣。

　　表達假設語氣的方法，第一是**if引導條件句**，這類條件句可以用來表達「條件式假設」以及「與事實相反的假設」；第二就是**用wish來**表達假設性的願望。

條件式假設

　　條件式假設通常用if來引導條件句。

1▶ 單純描述條件的假設

　　這類假設是用來表達「當條件成立，就會成為事實」，也就是有可能會發生的假設。

【基本句型】

If＋現在簡單式條件句＋主詞 $\begin{cases} \text{will} \\ \text{can} \\ \text{may} \\ \text{should} \\ \text{must} \\ ... \end{cases}$ ＋原形動詞

例1

If	you can give me a better price,	I	will	buy it.
If	現在簡單式條件句	主詞	助動詞	原形動詞

（如果你能給我一個更優惠的價錢，我就會買它。）

例2

If	we set off before eight,	we	shouldn't	be late.
If	現在簡單式條件句	主詞	助動詞	原形動詞

（如果我們八點之前出發，我們就不會遲到。）

【 特殊用法 】

除了if之外，可以引導單純條件子句的連接詞還有：

- **on condition that** （如果）
- **provided that / providing that**（倘若，以……為條件）
- **as long as / so long as**（只要）
- **in case (that)** （萬一）

例 • **Provided / Providing (that)** no objections are raised, we will consider the matter settled.
（假如沒有任何反對意見，我們就認定這件事情已經解決了。）

- You can apply for the scholarship **on condition that** you are a straight-A student.
（假如你是個成績全優等的學生，你就可以申請此獎學金。）

- **In case (that)** an earthquake occurs, don't use the elevator.
（萬一有地震發生，不要使用電梯。）

★ in case of 後面，也可以接名詞喔！例如：In case of an earthquake, don't use the elevator.

原來還能這樣說！

圈出正確的字，以完成句子

1. If you (follow / will follow) the instructions, you cannot go wrong.
2. As long as he (had / has) a correct map, he (should / could) be able to find the way to the hotel.
3. (On condition that / In case of) emergency, call me by this number.
4. If you (are willing to / will) give me a lift, I will be very grateful.
5. We can spend less time cleaning if we (move / moved) to a smaller house

ANSWER

1. follow	3. In case of	5. move
2. has ; should	4. are willing to	

2 與現在事實相反的假設

表達「與現在事實不符」的假設時，if引導的條件句必須「不是現在式」，因此要用「過去式」，來表示「它不是事實」。

【 基本句型 】

If＋過去簡單式條件句＋主詞 { would / could / might / should / … } ＋原形動詞

注意 因為條件與現在事實不符，主句所述一定不會成立，因此主句的助動詞也必須用過去式。

例1

If	I had a car,	I	would	drive you home.
If	過去簡單式條件句	主詞	助動詞	原形動詞

（如果我有車，我就會開車送你回家。）

例2

If	we spoke French,	we	should	be able to tell him what happened.
If	過去簡單式條件句	主詞	助動詞	原形動詞

（如果我們會說法文，我們就能告訴他發生了什麼事。）

【 be動詞用were 】

　　if子句中的動詞若為be動詞，無論人稱為何，都用were。

例 • If I **were** your father, I would be very proud of you.
（如果我是你父親，我將會非常以你為傲。）

• If Steve Jobs **were** still alive, what would he say?
（如果賈伯斯還在世的話，他會怎麼說？）

【表示強烈與事實相反的假設語氣的句型】

If＋主詞＋were to＋原形動詞,＋主詞 { would / could / might / should / ... } ＋原形動詞

例1

If	you	**were to**	**die**	tomorrow,	what	would	you	do?
If	主詞	were to	原形動詞			助動詞	主詞	原形動詞

（如果你明天就要死去，你會做什麼？）

例2

If	the sun	**were to**	**rise**	in the west	would	the world	be any different?
If	主詞	were to	原形動詞		助動詞	主詞	原形動詞

（如果太陽從西邊升起，世界會有什麼不同嗎？）

OH, no~

文法練習站 ❷

圈出正確的字，以完成句子

1. If he (has / had) a decent job and a steady income, he should be able to support his family.

2. If you (are / were) in my shoes, you wouldn't say that.

3. We could see each other every day if we (went / have gone) to the same school.

4. If my father (was / were) here, he would be as happy as we are.

5. If the sun (is / were) to rise in the west, it would be the end of the world.

ANSWER

1. had　　2. were　　3. went　　4. were　　5. were

3 與過去事實相反的假設

　　表達「與過去事實不符」的假設時，if引導的條件句必須「不是過去式」，因此要用「過去完成式」，來表示「它不是事實」。

【基本句型】

If＋過去完成式條件句,＋主詞 $\left\{\begin{array}{l}\text{would}\\\text{could}\\\text{might}\\\text{should}\\...\end{array}\right\}$ ＋have＋<u>過去分詞</u>

注意 因為條件與過去事實不符，主句所述在過去時間也一定不可能發生，因此主句也要改成「過去式助動詞＋ have+ V-p.p.」，表示「在過去沒有發生，未曾成立」。

例1

If	we had practiced harder,	we	wouldn't	have	lost the game.
If	過去完成式條件句,	主詞	助動詞	have	過去分詞

（如果我們練習得更努力一點，我們就不會輸掉比賽了。）

過去並沒有練習得更努力，所以已經輸掉比賽

例2

If	he had driven more carefully,	he	wouldn't	have	been killed in the car crash.
If	過去完成式條件句	主詞	助動詞	have	過去分詞

（如果他更小心開車，他就不會死於車禍）

他並沒有開得很小心，所以他已經死於車禍

 文法練習站 ❸

將提示字作適當修改，填入空格中，以完成句子

1. Mike has already left. If you _____ (arrive) earlier, you_____ _____ (can / meet) him.

2. I'm sorry that Mary died. She should _____ (avoid) the fatal disaster if she _____ (take) my advice.

3. Too bad that Jeff quit. If he _____ (not) quit, he _____ _____ (may be / promote) to the director of the branch office.

4. I used to be very good at doing business. I _____ (may be) a successful businesswoman if I _____ (not / be) married.

5. The couple bought a small apartment for themselves. If they _____ (have) children, they_____ (may / buy) a bigger house.

ANSWER

1. had arrived ; could have met
2. have avoided ; had taken
3. had not ; might have been promoted
4. might have been ; had bit been
5. had ; might have bought

4 與未來情況相反的假設

假設未來可能會發生的事情時，用if引導「希望不要發生」的未來條件。當事情很有可能發生時，主句的助動詞用will／can／should／may等＋原形動詞；當事情幾乎不可能發生時，主句的助動詞用would／could／should／might等＋原形動詞。

【基本句型】

If ＋ 主詞 ＋ should ＋ 原形動詞 ＋ 主詞 ＋ 助動詞 ＋ 原形動詞

例1

If	it	**should**	rain	tomorrow,	the outdoor party	**will**	be put off.
If	主詞	should	原形動詞		主詞	助動詞	原形動詞

（萬一明天下雨的話，戶外派對就會被延後舉行。）

明天可能下雨!? 派對可能會延後舉行!?

例2

If	she	**should**	be late	again,	she	**can**	be fired.
If	主詞	should	原形動詞		主詞	助動詞	原形動詞

（萬一她再次遲到，她可能就會被開除。）

她很有可能再遲到!? 她很可能被開除!?

【主句為「祈使句」】

以if＋should引導表示「萬一」的條件句，後面也可以接「祈使句」作主句。

例 • **If** there should be an emergency, press this button.
（萬一發生緊急事件，就按這個按鈕。）

主要子句用原形動詞開頭。

• **If** you should have any questions, please contact me.
（萬一你有任何問題，請與我聯絡。）

主要子句用原形動詞開頭。

【省略連接詞if】

當if所引導的假設條件為下列情況時，可以省略連接詞if，並將主詞與助動詞倒裝。

倒裝句變給你看

如要表達「如果她當時在這裡的話，問題就能被解決了。」
其中If子句原本是：

If she had been there then,
　　 主詞　 助動詞

the problem would have been solved.

辦辦　找來了~你可以下班了！

可以變成

Had she been here then,
助動詞　　主詞

the problem would have been solved.

就是If省略之後，主詞和助動詞換位置站！

再看看其他的例子吧！

與過去事實相反（had+V-p.p.）

例 If the rescue had not arrived in time, we would have been dead.

= If Had the rescue not arrived in time, we would have been dead.
（如果救援沒有及時趕到的話，我們可能已經死了。）

表示萬一（should）

例 If you should have any problems, please don't hesitate to let me know.

= If Should you have any problems, please don't hesitate to let me know.
（萬一你有任何問題，請儘管讓我知道。）

與現在事實相反的be動詞句型

例 If I were your mother, I wouldn't let you do that.

= If Were I your mother, I wouldn't let you do that.
（如果我是你媽媽，我不會讓你那麼做。）

文法練習站 ❹

圈出正確的字，以完成句子

1. Had he done it, he (should have / had had) run away.

2. (Should / Would) Mr. Jefferson call, tell him that I'm on leave today.

3. If it (could / should) rain this afternoon, I will pick you up at school.

4. If our flight (had been / should be) delayed, we would have missed the meeting.

5. If James (should / had) be late, wait for him.

 願望式假設

表達假設性的願望時，通常會用wish假設語氣來陳述一個不可能成真的願望，表示「要是……多好」。

1 與現在事實不符的假設願望

wish後以that引導過去式的子句，表示「現在不可能成真」。

【基本句型】

主詞＋wish (that) ＋主詞 ｛ were＋補語
過去式動詞
could / would＋原形動詞

表達與事實不符的願望時，無論主詞為何，be動詞一律用were

例1

She	**wishes**	she	were	thinner, younger and prettier.
主詞	wish(that)	主詞	were	補語

（她希望她能瘦一點、年輕一點、漂亮一點。）

可是她又胖又老又醜。

例2

I	**wish (that)**	I	had a car
主詞	wish(that)	主詞	過去式動詞

（我希望我有一台車。）

可是我現在沒車。

例3

We	**wish (that)**	we	could join you.
主詞	wish(that)	主詞	could / would＋原形動詞

（我們真希望能加入你們。）

可是我們無法加入你們。

2 與過去事實不符的假設願望

that引導過去完成式的句子，表示與過去事實不符。

【 基本句型 】

主詞＋wish (that) ＋過去完成式

例1

I	**wish (that)**	I had treated her better when she was alive.
主詞	wish (that)	過去完成式

（真希望她在世時，我有對她好一點。）

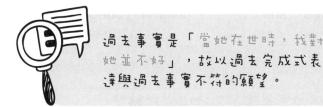

過去事實是「當她在世時，我對她並不好」，故以過去完成式表達與過去事實不符的願望。

例2

He	**wished (that)**	he had never made that silly mistake.
主詞	wish (that)	過去完成式

（他真希望他從未犯過那樣愚蠢的錯誤。）

過去事實是「他犯下了（令人不可置信的）愚蠢錯誤」，故以過去完成式表達與過去事實不符的願望。

原來如此！

★ wish與hope的差異

hope用來表達可能成真的「希望」；wish則是用來表達不可能成真的「願望」。

例1

I	hope	we	can	achieve our sales target this month.
我	希望	我們	（現在式助動詞）	這個月達成銷售目標。

→表示對未來的希望

例2

I	wish	we	had	achieved our sales target last month.
我	真希望	我們	（過去式助動詞）	上個月有達到銷售目標。

→表達與過去事實不符的假設性願望

例3

I	hope	you	can	stay longer.
我	希望	你	（現在式助動詞）能	待久一點。

→ 有可能成真的希望

例4

I	hope	we	could	stay longer.
我	希望	我們	（過去式助動詞）可以	待久一點。

→ 不可能成真的願望

文法練習站 ❺

圈出正確的字，以完成句子

1. I wish I (could / should) stay longer. Unfortunately, I really have to go now.

2. They wish they (practiced / had practiced) harder. If they did, they would have done better.

3. He wishes he (had seen / saw) a doctor earlier, so his cancer could have been discovered at an early stage.

4. She wishes that she (was / were) smarter, so she would learn things faster.

5. I wish I (had / had had) enough money to buy a large house, so that all my family could live together.

ANSWER

1. could	3. had seen	5. had
2. had practiced	4. were	

文法總複習

A 選擇

1. ( ) If he had asked me, I _____ him.
   A. would have helped　　B. will help
   C. could help　　D. should help

2. ( ) If you _____ now, we will come back later.
   A. were working　　B. have been working
   C. are working　　D. would have been working

3. ( ) If the weather _____ nice last weekend, they could have gone to the beach.
   A. was　　B. were　　C. has been　　D. had been

4. ( ) We _____ late for school if we hadn't missed the school bus.
   A. won't be　　B. wouldn't have been
   C. will be　　D. could have been

5. ( ) The man shouldn't have been dead if he _____ to the hospital earlier.
   A. would send　　B. could have been sent
   C. had been sent　　D. were sent

6. ( ) _____ we have spare money, can we buy a bike?
   A. Should　　B. Will　　C. Could　　D. Unless

7. ( ) I will go bungee jumping _____ you go too.
   A. should　　B. as long as　　C. until　　D. otherwise

8. ( ) _____ you pay for me, I won't be able to go on a cruise holiday.
   A. Provided that　　B. If　　C. As long as　　D. Unless

B 依提示改寫句子

Example: You need to have your parents' permission to marry at the age of 16.（providing that）

→*Providing that you have your parents' permission, you can get marry at the age of 16.*

1. It wasn't nice yesterday, so we didn't go picnicking. (if)

_____

2. Unless you stop screaming, I will leave now. (if)

_____

3. Jack doesn't have a steady income. Therefore Jenny wouldn't marry him. (providing)

_____

4. Joanna never had a health checkup, so she didn't know she was sick. (if)

_____

5. I am so busy now, so I can't go visit my grandparents. (if)

_____

6. I am not rich, so I can't help the poor. (wish)

_____

7. If he had been more careful, he wouldn't have had a car accident. (wish)

_____

ANSWER

A. 選擇

1. A   2. C   3. D   4. B   5. C   6. A   7. B   8. D

B. 依提示改寫句子

1. If it had been nice yesterday, we would have gone picnicking.
2. If you don't stop screaming, I will leave now.
3. If Jack had a steady income, Jenny would have married him.
4. If Joanna had had a health checkup, she would have known she was sick.
5. If I were not so busy now, I would go visit my grandparents.
6. I wish I were rich, so that I could help the poor.
7. He wishes that he had been more careful, so that he wouldn't have had a car accident.

Lesson 2

關係代名詞與子句 I

「那個戴眼鏡的女孩，是我的菜！」

The girl who wears glasses is my type.

關係代名詞與子句 I

英文中的連接詞，除了對等連接詞、相關連接詞以及附屬連接詞之外，還有一種同時具有代名詞性質，可以取代句子中的先行詞，引導一個關係子句來修飾先行詞的連接詞，這種連接詞，就是大家耳熟能詳的「關係代名詞」。這種可以在主句中形成複句的連接詞，在英文句型中非常重要，也相當常用，雖然文法句型有點複雜，但是要搞清楚也不是太難的事。只要按部就班跟著練習，就能所向披靡了。

關係代名詞

關係代名詞所引導的子句，是一個形容詞子句，目的是用來修飾關係代名詞前面的先行詞。

人稱關係代名詞有以下五個，可以用來取代不同的先行詞：

先行詞	主格	受格	所有格
人	who	whom	whose
事物；動物	which	which	X
人；事物；動物	that	that	X

關係代名詞除了是整個句子中，引導關係子句的「連接詞」，也是關係子句的主詞。因此關係子句由哪個關係代名詞來引導，必須先看關係子句所要修飾之先行詞是什麼，來決定要用「主格」、「受格」還是「所有格」。

1 限定關係子句

　　所謂「限定」就是明確指定所修飾的先行詞，因此who, which及that就是引導一個「限定關係子句」，用來描述所指稱的是「何人」或「何物」。

　　當關係子句所修飾的先行詞為人時，用「who」；先行詞為物時，用「which」；而「that」則是人或物皆可適用。

【who用來代替「人」】

例1

（我訪問了那個女子。）

I interviewed	the woman.	
	The woman	owned the restaurant.

（那個女子擁有這間餐廳。）

I interviewed the woman who owned the restaurant.

（我訪問了擁有這間餐廳的女子。）

第二個句子變成形容詞子句以修飾第一個句子，the woman 以關係代名詞 who 取代，引導出一個關係子句

原來如此！

例2

（那男子非常熱心。）

| The man | was very enthusiastic. |
| The man | volunteered to help the refugees. |

（那男子自願幫助難民。）

The man (who) volunteered to help the refugees was very enthusiastic. （那位自願幫助難民的男子非常熱心。）

第二個句子變成形容詞子句以修飾第一個句子，the man以關係代名詞who取代，引導出一個關係子句

原來如此！

【 which 用來代替「物」】

例1

（你完成指定作業了嗎？）

| Have you done | the assignment | ? |
| | The assignment | is supposed to be submitted next week. |

（這份作業應該要在下週繳交。）

Have you done the assignment (which) is supposed to be submitted next week?

（你完成了下星期要交的指定作業了嗎？）

第二個句子變成形容詞子句以修飾第一個句子，the assignment以關係代名詞which取代，引導出一個關係子句。

原來如此！

例2

（你把錢藏在哪裡？）

1. Where did you hide	the money	?
2. You stole	the money	from the old lady.

（你從老太太那裡偷了錢。）

請跟著步驟這樣做！

Step 1 ➡ 找出一樣的字「the money」。

句1 **Where did you hide** the money**?**
句2 **You stole** the money **from the old lady.**

Step 2 ➡ 把句2中「the money」換成關係代名詞「which」。

句2 **You stole** the money **from the old lady.**

You stole which **from the old lady.**

Step 3 ➡ 把句2中，把 which 這個字移到最前面。

句2 **You stole** which **from the old lady.**

Which you stole from the old lady.

Step 4 ➡ 把改造後的句2，緊接在句1的「the money」之後。

Where did you hide the money which
you stole from the old lady?

（你把從老太太那裡偷來的錢藏在哪裡？）

【that可以用來指「人」或「物」】

例1　（她決定跳槽到那間公司。）

She decided to job-hop to	the company.	
	The company	offered her a higher salary.

（那間公司提供她更高的薪水。）

She decided to job-hop to the company that offered her a higher salary.

（她決定跳槽到那間提供她更高薪水的公司。）

第二個句子變成形容詞子句以修飾第一個句子，the company可以用關係代名詞that取代，引導出一個關係子句。

原來如此！

例2　（警察阻止了那個男子。）

The security guard stopped	the man.	
	The man	tried to break into the building.

（男子企圖強行進入大樓。）

The security guard stopped the man that tried to break into the building.

（警衛阻止了企圖強行進入大樓的男子。）

第二個句子中的the man可以用關係代名詞that取代，引導出一個關係子句，修飾第一個句子。

原來如此！

Lesson 1

Lesson 2

Lesson 3

Lesson 4

Lesson 5

Lesson 6

Lesson 7

Lesson 8

Lesson 9

Lesson 10

文法練習站 ❶

以關係代名詞合併句子

1. Mary is going to job-hop to the company. The company offers her a better salary. _____

   _____

2. They sold the apartment. The apartment is located in downtown area.

   _____

   _____

3. We're going to be late for the concert. The concert starts at 7o'clock.

   _____

   _____

4. Have you met the young woman? The young woman volunteered to look after the old lady.

   _____

   _____

5. My dad is marrying a woman. The woman is five years younger than me

   _____

   _____

ANSWER

1. Mary is going to job-hop to the company which/that offers her a better salary.
2. They sold the apartment which/that is located in downtown area.
3. We're going to be late for the concert which/that starts at 7 o'clock.
4. Have you met the young woman who/that volunteered to look after the old lady?
5. My dad is marrying a woman who/that is five years younger than me.

【省略關係代名詞】

　　當限定關係子句所修飾的先行詞為受格時，關係代名詞可以省略。

◆ 1. whom用來代替「人」

例1　　（我們正在談論那個女孩。）

1. We are talking about	the girl.	
2. Jeffery introduced	the girl	to me last night.

（Jeffery昨晚介紹那個女孩給我。）

請跟著步驟這樣做！

Step 1 ➡ 找出一樣的字「**the girl**」。

句1 **We are talking about** the girl.
句2 **Jeffery introduced** the girl **to me last night.**

Step 2 ➡ 把句2中「**the girl**」換成關係代名詞「**whom**」。

句2 **Jeffery introduced** ~~the girl~~ **to me last night.**

Jeffery introduced whom **to me last night.**

Step 3 ➡ 把句2中，把**whom**這個字移到最前面。

句2 **Jeffery introduced** whom **to me last night.**

Whom Jeffery introduced to me last night.

Step 4 ➡️ 把改造後的句2，緊接在句1的「**the girl**」之後。

We are talking about the girl whom Jeffery introduced to me last night.

（我們正在談論昨晚Jeffery介紹給我認識的女孩。）

第二個句子中的the man用關係代名詞whom取代，引導出關係子句修飾第一個句子。由於關係代名詞為受詞，因此在關係子句中可以省略。

原來如此！

例2

（那男人似乎最能勝任這份工作。）

1.	The man	seems the most qualified to do the job.
2. We interviewed	the man	yesterday.

（我們昨天面試那個男子。）

請跟著步驟這樣做！

Step 1 ➡️ 找出一樣的字「**the man**」。

句1 The man **seems the most qualified to do the job.**
句2 We interviewed the man **yesterday.**

Step 2 ➡️ 把句2中「**the man**」換成關係代名詞「**whom**」。

句2 We interviewed the man yesterday.

We interviewed whom yesterday.

Step 3 ➡️ 把句2中，把 **whom** 這個字移到最前面。

句2 We interviewed (whom) yesterday.

Whom we interviewed yesterday.

Step 4 ➡️ 把改造後的句2，緊接在句1的「**the girl**」之後。

The man (whom) we interviewed yesterday seems the most qualified to do the job.

（我們昨天面試的那個男子似乎最能勝任這份工作。）

◆ 2. which用來代替「物」

例1   （這張餐桌是大理石做的。）

1.	The dining table	is made of marble.
2. My grandfather bought	this dining table	twenty years ago.

（我爺爺在二十年前買了這張餐桌。）

請跟著步驟這樣做！

Step 1 ➡️ 找出一樣的字「**the dining table**」。

句1 The dining table is made of marble.
句2 My grandfather bought this dining table twenty years ago.

Step 2 ➡️ 把句2中「**the dining table**」換成關係代名詞「**which**」。

句2 My grandfather bought ~~this dining table~~ twenty years ago.

My grandfather bought which twenty years ago.

Step 3 把句2中，把 **which** 這個字移到最前面。

句2 My grandfather bought which twenty years ago.

Which my grandfather bought twenty years ago.

Step 4 把改造後的句2，緊接在句1的「**the dining table**」之後。

The dining table which my grandfather bought twenty years ago is made of marble.

（我爺爺在二十年前買的這張餐桌是用大理石做的。）

> 第二個句子變成形容詞子句以修飾第一個句子，the dining table可以用關係代名詞which取代，引導出一個關係子句。由於which在此為受詞，因此在關係子句中可以省略。

原來如此！

例2 （你有看到那個牛皮紙袋嗎？）

1. Have you seen	the brown paper bag	?
2. I put	It (the brown paper bag)	on my desk.

（我把它放在我桌上。）

請跟著步驟這樣做！

Step 1 找出一樣的字「**the brown paper bag**」。

句1 **Have you seen** the brown paper bag **?**
句2 **I put It (**the brown paper bag**) on my desk.**

Step 2 ➡ 把句2中「**the brown paper bag**」（或代名詞 **it**）
換成關係代名詞「**which**」。

句2 I put It (the brown paper bag) on my desk.

⬇

I put which on my desk.

Step 3 ➡ 把句2中，把**which** 這個字移到最前面。

句2 I put (which) on my desk.

⬇

Which I put on my desk.

Step 4 ➡ 把改造後的句2，緊接在句1的
「**the brown paper bag**」之後。

Have you seen the brown paper bag (which)
I put on my desk?（你有看到我放在我桌上的那個牛皮紙袋嗎？）

◆ 3. that可以用來代替「人」或「物」

例　　（這就是那本書。）

| 1. This is | the book. | |
| 2. I have been reading | this book | for a long time. |

（我已經讀這本書很久了。）

請跟著步驟這樣做！

Lesson 1
Lesson 2
Lesson 3
Lesson 4
Lesson 5
Lesson 6
Lesson 7
Lesson 8
Lesson 9
Lesson 10

Step 1 找出一樣的對象「the book」、「this book」。

句1 **This is** the book.

句2 **I have been reading** this book **for a long time.**

Step 2 把句2中「this book」換成關係代名詞「that」。

句2 **I have been reading** this book **for a long time.**

I have been reading that **for a long time.**

Step 3 把句2中，把 that 這個字移到最前面。

句2 **I have been reading** that **for a long time.**

That **I have reading for a long time.**

Step 4 把改造後的句2，緊接在句1的「the book」之後。

This is the book that **I have been reading for a long time.** （這就是那本我已經找了很久的書。）

第二個句子中的the book可以用關係代名詞that取代，引導出關係子句修飾第一個句子。由於that在此為受詞，因此在關係子句中可以省略。

原來如此！

以關係代名詞合併句子

1. He sold the farm. He inherited the farm from his father.

   _____

   _____

2. Maria is the woman. I want to spend the rest of my life with the woman. _____

   _____

3. Mom is reading the book. I borrowed the book from the library.

   _____

   _____

4. The money has disappeared. She put the money on the table.

   _____

   _____

5. Josh is the new bodyguard. Mr. Cooper hired a new bodyguard to protect him 24/7.

   _____

   _____

ANSWER

1. He sold the farm (which / that) he inherited from his father.
2. Maria is the woman (that) I want to spend the rest of my life with.
3. Mom is reading the book (which / that) I borrowed from the library.
4. The money (which / that) she put on the table has disappeared.
5. Josh is the new bodyguard (that) Mr. Cooper hired to protect him 24 / 7.

【 whose 作為所有格關係代名詞 】

當限定關係子句所修飾的先行詞為所有格時，whose可以取代「人」的所有格，作為關係子句的連接詞。

例1　　（那男子很著急。）

1. The man	is anxious.	
2. The man's	money	has been stolen.

（男子的錢被偷了。）

請跟著步驟這樣做！

Step 1 ➡ 找出一樣的對象「The man」、「The man's」。

句1 The man is anxious.
句2 The man's money has been stolen.

Step 2 ➡ 把句2中「The man」寫成所有格「The man's」
→換成所有格關係代名詞「whose」。

句2 ~~The man's~~ money has been stolen.

whose money has been stolen.

Step 3 ➡ 把改造後的句2，緊接在句1的「The man」之後。

The man (whose) money has been stolen is anxious.

（那個錢被偷走的男子非常著急。）

第二個句子中的the man's可以用關係代名詞whose取代，引導出關係子句修飾第一個句子。

原來如此！

例2　（這些人都是詐騙的受害者。）

1. These people		are all victims of fraud.
2. Their (These people's)	savings had been raided.	

（他們的積蓄已經被洗劫一空。）

請跟著步驟這樣做！

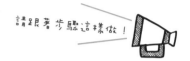

Step 1 ➡️ 找出一樣的對象「**These people**」、「**Their**」。

句1 These people **are all victims of fraud.**
句2 Their (These people's) **savings had been raided.**

Step 2 ➡️ 把句2中「**These people**」寫成所有格 「**Their**」，代表「**These people's**」→換成所有格關係代名詞「**whose**」。

~~**句2** Their (These people's) **savings had been raided.**~~
↓
whose **savings had been raided.**

Step 3 ➡️ 把改造後的句2，緊接在句1的「**These people**」之後。

These people (whose) savings had been raided
are all victims of fraud.

（這些積蓄已經被洗劫一空的人都是詐騙的受害者。）

改造句子
大功告成

文法練習站 ❸

以關係代名詞合併句子

1. I've got a friend. His father is a prestigious cardiologist.

   _____

   _____

2. He is the man. His house got broken into.

   _____

   _____

3. Jenny is the candidate. Her qualifications successfully meet all our requirements.

   _____

   _____

4. Chopin is a great musician. His works of music are world-famous.

   _____

   _____

5. The scholar is very angry. Her thesis was plagiarized.

   _____

   _____

ANSWER

1. I've got a friend whose father is a prestigious cardiologist.
2. He is the man whose house got broken into.
3. Jenny is the candidate whose qualifications successfully meet all our requirements.
4. Chopin is a great musician whose works of music are world-famous.
5. The scholar whose thesis was plagiarized is very angry.

66 關係代名詞只能用that的情況 99

一般來說，使用who、whom及which的關係子句也可以用that取代作為關係代名詞，但是以下狀況的關係子句，只能用that作為關係代名詞，

❶ 先行詞中有最高級或序數

例 • Elaine is **the most thoughtful girl** that I have ever met.
（Elaine是我認識的女生中最善解人意的。）

the most thoughtful→形容詞最高級

• This is **the last time** that I will lend you money.
（這是我最後一次借錢給你。）

the last→序數

❷ 先行詞中有強調語氣如the very, the only

例 • John is **the very boyfriend** that you wish you could have.
（John就是那種你會希望可以擁有的男朋友。）

• You are **the only person** that I could trust.
（你是我唯一可以信任的人。）

❸ 先行詞中有表示全部語詞的形容詞all, every, each

例 • This is **all** that I can do for you.
（這是我可以為你做的所有事了。）

• I can still remember **every word** that you said on that day.
（我仍記得你那天所說的每一句話。）

❹ 先行詞同時包含人及動物時

例 • **The woman and the cat** that walked into the forest were never seen again.

（再也沒有人見過走進森林裡的女子和貓。）

• The police found **the old man and the old dog** that lived in the cabin dead.

（警方發現住在小屋的老人與老狗已經死了。）

❺ 先行詞為be動詞補語時

例 • Emma is **the girl** that Kevin has been talking about.

（Emma就是Kevin一直在談論的那個女孩。）

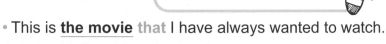

the girl ＝主詞Emma的補語

• This is **the movie** that I have always wanted to watch.

（這就是那部我一直想看的電影。）

the movie ＝主詞this的補語

文法練習站 ❹

請在正確位子填入關係代名詞

1. This is the very opportunity you should seize if you want to succeed. _____
_____

2. This is the watch I've been looking for. Where did you find it?
_____
_____

3. The little girl and the puppy are walking toward us live next to me.
_____
_____

4. Toy Story is one of the most interesting movies I've watched so far.
_____
_____

5. Today is the last day Mr. Robinson works with us. He is retiring tomorrow. _____
_____

ANSWER

1. This is the very opportunity that you should seize if you want to succeed.
2. This is the watch that I've been looking for. Where did you find it?
3. The little girl and the puppy that are walking toward us live next to me.
4. Toy Story is one of the most interesting movies that I've watched so far.
5. Today is the last day that Mr. Robinson works with us. He is retiring tomorrow.

2 非限定關係子句

不同於「限定關係子句」中who, which及that明確指定所修飾的先行詞，在非限定關係子句中，關係子句並無法明確指定所修飾的是哪些人或物，只能提供更多有關他們的資訊。

非限定關係子句通常以逗號與前後句子隔開，並且人只能用who代表，物只能用which代表，不能用that，而且關係代名詞不能省略。

【who代替「人」】

例1

（Josephine現在住在紐約的妹妹，最近剛結婚。）

 由先行詞已經知道所談論的是Josephine的妹妹，who is living in New York只是提供更多有關這個人的訊息，並無法幫助我們知道此人是誰。

例2

（昨晚我遇到John，他告訴我他辭去工作了。）

【which代替「物」】

例1　（奶奶給我一條項鍊，我把它放在珠寶盒裡。）

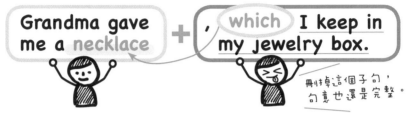

例2　（Melisa繼承了她父親市值一百萬美元的房子。）

【whose代替「人的所有格」】

例1　（Tina Brown是我的一個好朋友。）

1. Tina Brown		is a good friend of mine.
2. Her (Tina Brown's)	brother	is the popular singer Tim Brown.

（Tina Brown的哥哥是名歌手。）

請跟著步驟這樣做！

Step 1 ➡ 找出一樣的對象「**Tina Brown**」、「**Her**」。

句1 Tina Brown is a good friend of mine.

句2 Her (Tina Brown's) brother is the popular singer Tim Brown.

Step 2 ⟹ 把句2中「Tina Brown」寫成所有格「Her」，代表「Tina Brown's」→換成所有格關係代名詞「whose」。

句2 Her (Tina Brown's) brother is the popular singer Tim Brown.

whose brother is the popular singer Tim Brown.

Step 3 ⟹ 把改造後的句2，緊接在句1的「Tian Brown」之後。

Tina Brown , ⟨whose⟩ brother is the popular singer Tim Brown, is a good friend of mine.

（Tina Brown，她哥哥是名歌手Tim Brown，是我的一個好朋友。）

例2　（我的朋友Lily花錢如流水。）

1. **My friend Lily**		spends money like water.
2. **Her (My friend Lily's)**	husband is a successful businessman	

（Lily的先生是一個成功的生意人。）

My friend Lily, ⟨whose⟩ husband is a successful businessman, spends money like water.

（我的朋友莉莉，她先生是一個成功的生意人，花錢如流水。）

改造句子
大功告成

★ 比較限定關係子句與非限定關係子句的不同

例1【非限定】

Grandma gave me a necklace, <u>which</u> I keep in my jewelry box.

（奶奶給我一條項鍊，我把它放在珠寶盒裡。）

→非限定關係子句無法使人明確辨認所說的項鍊是哪一條。

【限定】

The necklace <u>which</u> I keep in my jewelry box is a gift from Grandma.

（我放在珠寶盒裡的項鍊是奶奶送的禮物。）

→限定關係子句可使人明確知道所說的項鍊是放在珠寶盒裡的那一條。

例1【非限定】

Chloe's mother, <u>who</u> is 45, looks as young as she does.

（Chloe四十五歲的母親，看起來就跟她一樣年輕。）

→非限定關係子句目的在提供有關先行詞的更多資訊。

【限定】

The woman <u>who</u> is 45 years old is Chloe's mother.

（那個四十五歲的女人就是Chloe的媽媽。）

→限定關係子句可使人明確知道所指的女子是哪一個。

文法練習站 ⑤

以連接詞合併句子

1. Jonathan speaks excellent English. Jonathan has only learned English for two years. _____
_____

2. Mary's brother didn't want to go with us. He is not very interested in shopping. _____
_____

3. My grandma still exercises every day. She is 85 years old.
_____
_____

4. Liverpool is the hometown of the Beatles. It is about 178 miles from London. _____
_____

5. This is the parcel. The parcel came this morning.
_____
_____

ANSWER

1. Jonathan, who has only learned English for two years, speaks excellent English.
2. Mary's brother, who is not very interested in shopping, didn't want to go with us.
3. My grandma, who is 85 years old, still exercises every day.
4. Liverpool, which is about 178 miles from London, is the hometown of the Beatles.
5. This is the parcel that came this morning.

Lesson 2

文法總複習

A 選擇

1. (　) This is the painting _____ our teacher mentioned several times in the art class.
   A. who   B. whose
   C. that   D. whom

2. (　) What is the name of the company _____ you work for?
   A. that   B. whose
   C. whom   D. who

3. (　) I would like to return a sweater _____ I bought two days ago.
   A. X   B. who
   C. whom   D. whose

4. (　) The waiter _____ served us wasn't very patient.
   A. whom   B. which
   C. whose   D. that

5. (　) Gill, _____ attitude at work had been unsatisfactory, was fired last week.
   A. that   B. which
   C. whose   D. whom

6. (　) Have you found the money _____ you lost?
   A. whom   B. that
   C. whose   D. who

7. (　) The man _____ interviewed me was very nice.
   A. whom   B. who
   C. which   D. whose

B 填空：填入which, who, whom, whose或that

1. Tom's parents, _____ are both retired, now live in San Francisco.

2. That is the most hilarious joke _____ I have ever heard.

3. The only person _____ I could trust in this world is myself.

4. My classmate Jack, _____ father is a diplomat, has been to over twenty countries since he was born.

5. My mother's office, _____ is located in downtown area, is only three blocks from the train station.

6. Our schoolmate Louisa, _____ is living in London with her husband, is expecting her third child.

7. The young man _____ we interviewed this morning has five years' managerial experience.

8. Mr. and Mrs. Peterson were the couple _____ son was badly injured in the accident.

Lesson 1
Lesson 2
Lesson 3
Lesson 4
Lesson 5
Lesson 6
Lesson 7
Lesson 8
Lesson 9
Lesson 10

ANSWER

A. 選擇

1. C 2. A 3. A 4. D 5. C 6. B 7. B

B. 依提示改寫句子

1. who	4. whose	7. whom
2. that	5. which	8. whose
3. that	6. who	

Lesson 3

關係代名詞
與子句Ⅱ

Lesson 3

> 「轉角的那間咖啡店，是我和她相遇的地方。」
> The café at the corner is the place I first met her.

關係代名詞與子句 II

在Lesson2中，我們已經知道關係代名詞可以引導出一個修飾先行詞的形容詞子句，並且有明確指定所修飾的人或物為何的「限定關係子句」，以及無法明確表示所修飾的人或物為何，卻能提供更多有關資訊的「非限定關係子句」兩種方式。

本章節將繼續介紹關係代名詞與子句，說明關係子句中有介系詞時，介系詞與關係代名詞之間的關係；以及除了who, which, whom, whose與that這五個關係代名詞之外，同樣可以用來引導出關係子句來修飾先行詞的關係副詞：where, when, why及how。

此外，複合關係代名詞如whoever, whatever等，也會在本章節一併介紹。

有介系詞的關係子句

1 限定關係子句

關係子句中的動詞為不及物動詞時，後面常需要介系詞接受詞，因此介系詞不可省略，但是可以移到關係代名詞（受詞）前。

例1

Mr. Smith is a customer		whom	you would never want to	deal	with.
Mr. Smith is a customer	with	whom	you would never want to	deal.	

（Mr. Smith是一個你永遠不想碰到的顧客。）

deal with（處理）片語中的介係詞可以移到 whom 之前。

原來如此！

例2

We visited the house		which	Shakespeare was	born	in.
We visited the house	in	which	Shakespeare was	born.	

（我們參觀了莎士比亞出生的房子。）

介係詞 in 可以移到 which 之前

原來如此！

　　有介系詞的關係子句，其關係代名詞通常是受詞，因此關係代名詞可省略，但是當介系詞放在關係代名詞前時，關係代名詞不可省略。

例1

We met the woman		(whom)	you talked	about	this morning.
We met the woman	about	whom	you talked		this morning.

（我們遇到你今天上午談到的那個女子。）

介係詞about可以移到 whom 之前

原來如此！

例2

The restaurant	(which)		we dined	in	last night is quite satisfactory.
The restaurant	in	which	we dined		last night is quite satisfactory.

（我們昨晚用餐的那家餐廳相當令人滿意。）

介係詞 in 可以移到 which 之前

2 非限定關係子句

在非限定關係子句中的介系詞同樣可以移到關係代名詞前，但是要注意的是，非限定關係子句中的關係代名詞不可省略。

例1

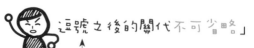

逗號之後的關代不可省略

Bill is studying geology	, which	I know very little	about.
Bill is studying geology	, about	which	I know very little.

（Bill在研究地質學，對此我所知甚少。）

介係詞 about 可以移到逗號之後、which 之前

例1

「逗號之後的關代不可省略」

James	, whom	we spent our holiday	with	, lives in Birmingham.
James	, with	whom	we spent our holiday	, lives in Birmingham.

（James，我們跟他一起度假的人，住在伯明罕。）

原來如此！

介係詞 with 可以移到逗號之後、whom 之前

【 指示代名詞＋of＋關係代名詞的關係子句句構 】

$$\left.\begin{array}{l} \text{some} \\ \text{many} \\ \text{much} \\ \text{none} \\ \text{all} \\ \text{...} \end{array}\right\} \text{of} + \text{which / whom}$$

例1　　（我有很多家人會來參加我的畢業典禮。）

1.		A number of my family	will attend my graduation ceremony.
2. You have met	some of	them	before.

（你以前已經見過他們其中一些。）

請跟著步驟這樣做！

061

Step 1 ➡ 找出同樣的名詞→ 句1的「**a number of my family**」和句2的「**them**」是同樣的人。

句1 A number of my family will attend my graduation ceremony.

句2 You have met <u>some of</u> them before.

Step 2 ➡ 把句2中「**them**」換成關係代名詞「**whom**」，接在修飾它的詞「**some of**」之後。

句2 You have met <u>some of</u> ~~them~~ before.

You have met <u>some of</u> whom before.

Step 3 ➡ 把句2的 **some of whom** 移到最前面。

句2 You have met some of whom before.

<u>some of</u> whom you have met before.

Step 4 ➡ 把改造後的句2，緊接在句1的「**A number of my family**」之後。

A number of my family, some of whom you have met before, will attend my graduation ceremony.

（我有很多家人，其中一些你以前已經見過，會來參加我的畢業典禮。）

原來如此！

非限定的關係子句，要加逗號喔！

例2 （我們收到很多意見。）

1. We received	a lot of comments.	
2. Most of	them	were very constructive.

（它們大部分都非常有建設性。）

請跟著步驟這樣做！

Step 1 ⟹ 找出同樣的名詞→ 句1的「**a lot of comments.**」和句2的「**them**」是同樣的人。

句1 **We received** a lot of comments.
句2 **Most of** them **were very constructive.**

Step 2 ⟹ 把句2中「**them**」換成關係代名詞「**which**」，接在修飾它的詞「**Most of**」之後。

句2 **Most of** them **were very constructive.**

Most of which **were very constructive.**

Step 4 ⟹ 把改造後的句2，緊接在句1的「**a lot of comments**」之後。

We received a lot of comments, most of which **were very constructive.**

（我們收到很多意見，其中大部份都非常有建設性。）

原來如此！

非限定的關係子句，只是補充說明的作用～

將介系詞＋關係代名詞填入空格中，以完成句子

with whom	under which	in which
about which	of which	

1. There are many dogs, most ＿＿＿＿＿＿ were abandoned, in the animal shelter.

2. The people ＿＿＿＿＿＿ I worked were very kind to me.

3. They were talking about astronomy, ＿＿＿＿＿＿ I hardly know anything.

4. My mom wanted me to learn the piano, ＿＿＿＿＿＿ I'm not really interested.

5. I can't believe we are standing on the ground ＿＿＿＿＿＿ Mozart was buried.

ANSWER

1. of which	3. about which	5. under which
2. with whom	4. in which	

關係副詞引導關係子句

除了關係代名詞之外，關係副詞也可用來引導關係子句修飾先行詞。

1 where 代表「地方」

關係副詞where引導一個表示「地點」、「位置」的形容詞子句，是由「介系詞＋which」變化而來，如in which, at which, on which或是under which等等。

【限定關係子句】

例1

Taipei is	**the city**	in which	I was born and raised.
Taipei is	**the city**	where	I was born and raised.

（台北是我出生及成長的城市。）

in which 變成關係副詞 where 了！

原來如此！

例2

He removed	**the sofa**	under which	the dog hid.
He removed	**the sofa**	where	the dog hid.

（他搬開那個狗狗躲在下面的沙發。）

under which 變成關係副詞 where 了！

原來如此！

【非限定關係子句】

例1

I went into	**a convenience store**	, in which	there were many customers.
I went into	**a convenience store**	, where	there were many customers.

（我走進一間裡面有很多顧客的便利商店。）

in which 變成關係副詞 where 了！

原來如此！

例2

| She waited at | **the taxi stand** | , at which | there was a long queue. |
| She waited at | **the taxi stand** | , where | there was a long queue. |

（她在排了一長條人龍的計程車站等著。）

at which 變成關係副詞 where 了！

Tips

★ 當 where 所修飾的先行詞為 be 動詞的補語時，可以將先行詞省略，保留關係副詞 where。

重點筆記

the place 是 be 動詞 is 的補語，可以省略。

例 That's **the place** where he was buried.

＝That's **where** he was buried.

（他就是被埋在那個地方。）

文法練習站 ❷

以 where 重寫句子

1. The dog waited at the spot at which he was abandoned by his owner. _____

   _____

2. That's the place at which the president got assassinated.

   _____

3. We dined in the restaurant in which my husband asked me to marry him. _____

   _____

4. He went back to the station at which he lost his wallet.

_____

5. Let's meet at the coffee shop at which we always have lunch.

_____

ANSWER

1. The dog waited at the spot where he was abandoned by his owner.
2. That's the place where the president got assassinated.
3. We dined in the restaurant where my husband asked me to marry him.
4. He went back to the station where he lost his wallet.
5. Let's meet at the coffee shop where we always have lunch.

2 when 代表「時間」

關係副詞when引導一個表示「時間」的形容詞子句,是由「介系詞＋which」變化而來,如at which, in which, by which等等。

【限定關係子句】

例1

That was	**the day**	on which	I met your mother.
That was	**the day**	when	I met your mother.

(那就是我認識你母親的日子。)

本來是on that day,變成on which、又簡化成關係副詞 when 了!

原來如此!

例2

Six thirty is usually	**the time**	at which	we have our dinner.
Six thirty is usually	**the time**	when	we have our dinner.

（六點半通常是我們吃晚飯的時間。）

進化史：at six thirty → at which → when

【非限定關係子句】

例1

Zack was born in	**March**	, in which	the cherry blossom festival just started.
Zack was born in	**March**	, when	the cherry blossom festival just started.

（Zack出生在三月，櫻花季正開始時。）

原本被合併的句子是「The cherry blossom festival just started in March」，被合併後，變成「in which」，又進化成關係副詞「when」了！

例2

Mom always gets up at	**4:30**	, at which	we are still in our dreams.
Mom always gets up at	**4:30**	, when	we are still in our dreams.

（媽媽總是在四點半起床，那時我們都仍還在睡夢中。）

進化史：at 4:30 → at which → when

Tips

★ 當 where 所修飾的先行詞為 be 動詞的補語時，可以將先行詞省略，保留關係副詞 where。

重點筆記

the day 是 be 動詞的補語，可省略。

例 That's **the day** when the school begins.
　＝That's **when** the school begins.
　（學校就是在那時候開學。）

以 when 重寫句子

1. That's the day on which my ex-girlfriend broke up with me.
　_____

2. You need to finish the work by next Friday, on which my boss will come back. _____
　_____

3. Mike usually comes home after 10 o'clock, at which all his children are already asleep. _____
　_____

4. I refuse to work on the weekend during which everyone else is on holiday. _____
　_____

5. I became a father the day on which you were born.
　_____

ANSWER

1. That's the day when my ex-girlfriend broke up with me.
2. You need to finish the work by next Friday, when my boss will come back.
3. Mike usually comes home after 10 o'clock, when all his children are already asleep.
4. I refuse to work on the weekend, when everyone else is on holiday.
5. I became a father the day when you were born.

3 why代表「原因」

關係副詞why引導一個表示「理由」的形容詞子句，只修飾the reason這個先行詞，是由「for＋which」變化而來，意指「因為某原因」。

★描述「原因」的形容詞子句，多為限定用法，很少用在非限定關係子句中。

例1

| I don't know | **the reason** | for which | they broke up. |
| I don't know | **the reason** | why | they broke up. |

（我不知道他們為了什麼原因分手。）

原本被合併的句子是They broke up for the reason.，被合併後，變成for which，又進化成關係副詞 why 了！

原來如此！

070

例2

We believed money was	**the reason**	for which	his wife left him.
We believed money was	**the reason**	why	his wife left him.

（我們認為錢是他的妻子離開他的原因。）

進化史：for the reason → for which → why

原來如此！

Tips

★當 why 所修飾的先行詞為 be 動詞的補語時，可以將先行詞省略，保留關係副詞 why。

重點筆記

the reason 是 be 動詞的補語，可省略。

例 That's **the reason** why I am here.
＝That's why I am here.
（這就是為什麼我會在這裡的原因。）

🚩 文法練習站 ❹

以 why 重寫句子

1. Constant lateness at work was the reason for which Jack got fired. _____

_____

2. Severe depression is believed to be the reason for which Robin Williams took his own life.

_____

_____

3. Overwork should be the reason for which he had a heart attack.

_____

_____

4. Health issue was the reason for which Mr. Wang resigned his job.

_____

_____

5. Drunk-driving was the reason for which this car accident occurred.

_____

_____

ANSWER

1. Constant lateness at work was the reason why Jack got fired.
2. Severe depression is believed to be the reason why Robin Williams took his own life.
3. Overwork should be the reason why he had a heart attack.
4. Health issue was the reason why Mr. Wang resigned his job.
5. Drunk-driving was the reason why this car accident occurred.

4 how代表「方式」

關係副詞how引導一個表示「方法」的形容詞子句，只用來修飾the way這個先行詞，是由「in＋which」變化而來，意指「以某種方法」。

★描述「方式」的形容詞子句，多為限定用法，很少用在非限定關係子句中。

★在表示「方法」的關係子句中，介系詞＋關係代名詞in which可以省略不用，或是以how完整取代the way in which ...，而不是只取代in which，因此the way後面不能接how關係子句。

例1

That's normally	**the way**	(in which)	we deal with customer complaints.
That's normally		how	we deal with customer complaints.

（那通常是我們處理顧客投訴的方式。）

NG寫法：

✗ That's normally ~~the way~~ how we deal with customer complaints.

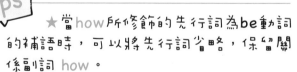

the way與how擇一使用在句子中！

請注意！

Tips　重點筆記

★當how所修飾的先行詞為be動詞的補語時，可以將先行詞省略，保留關係副詞 how。

the way是be動詞的補語，可省略。

例 That was **the way** he solved the problem.
　＝That was how he solved the problem.
　（他就是那樣解決問題的。）

文法練習站 ❺

以how重寫句子

1. I was pretty angry when I saw the way in which he treated his dog.

2. Sorting and recycling is the way we reduce the garbage.

3. Don't talk to me the way you talk to your children.

4. The way in which this restaurant handles customer complaints is inacceptable.

5. I think the way in which they won the game was really disgraceful.

ANSWER

1. I was pretty angry when I saw how he treated his dog.
2. Sorting and recycling is how we reduce the garbage.
3. Don't talk to me how you talk to your children.
4. The way in which this restaurant handles customer complaints is inacceptable.
5. I think the way in which they won the game was really disgraceful.

5 關係副詞的省略

在非限定關係子句中，關係副詞與關係代名詞一樣，是不可省略的。但在限定關係子句中，有些關係副詞是可以省略的。

where 不可省略	when 可以省略
how 必須省略	why 可以省略

【 where不可省略 】

例1

That's	**the country**	where	I am from.

（我就是來自這個國家。）

例2

I am positive (that) this is	**the place**	where	I put my passport.

（我肯定我就是把護照放在這個地方。）

【 when可以省略 】

例1

How could you forget	**the date**	(when)	we got married?

（你怎麼能忘記我們結婚的日子？）

例2

Tomorrow is	**the day**	(when)	he's leaving.

（明天就是他要離開的日子。）

【 why可以省略 】

例1

I'm sure that's	**the reason**	(why)	they chose you.

（我相信那就是他們選擇你的原因。）

例2

Do you know	**the reason**	(why)	she quitted?

（你知道她為什麼辭職嗎？）

【how一定要省略】

例1

ㄎ the way 就不需要找了！

The way	~~how~~	he takes care of his mother impressed me profoundly.

（他照顧母親的方式深深地感動了我。）

例2

ㄎ the way 就不需要找了！

I admire	The way	~~how~~	he treats his enemies.

（我欣賞他對待敵人的方式。）

文法練習站 ❻

判斷句子正確與否。正確的句子寫T（True），錯誤的句子寫F（False）

1. _____ Germany is the country Albert Einstein was born.
2. _____ Yesterday was the day my little brother graduated
3. _____ Going to the gym regularly is the way how she keeps fit.
4. _____ No one knows exactly why she committed suicide.
5. _____ Laziness is the reason he failed.

ANSWER
1. F   2. T   3. F   4. T   5. T

 複合關係代名詞

　　複合關係代名詞是由關係代名詞（如who）字尾加上 –ever所構成。在句子中同時具有先行詞與關係代名詞的功能，因此使用複合關係代名詞不需要先行詞。

1 whoever指「無論誰」

　　whoever為who+ever所組成的複合關係代名詞，可以用來取代「先行詞anyone＋關係代名詞who / that」，在關係子句中做主詞。

例1

I welcome	**anyone who**	volunteers to help.
I welcome	**whoever**	volunteers to help.

（我歡迎任何自願來幫忙的人。）

 原來如此！

anyone who可以代換成whoever

 主詞　　 關係子句

例2

Anyone who	**smuggles drugs into this country**	will be sentenced to death.
Whoever	**smuggles drugs into this country**	will be sentenced to death.

（無論誰走私毒品進入這個國家都會被判死刑。）

 原來如此！

anyone who跟whoever，後面都是接第三人稱單數動詞喔！

2 whomever 指「無論誰」（受格）

whomever為whom+ever所組成的複合關係代名詞，可以用來取代「先行詞anyone＋關係代名詞whom / that」，在關係子句中做受詞。

例1

You can invite	anyone whom	you like to the party.
You can invite	whomever	you like to the party.

（你可以邀請任何你喜歡的人來派對。）

anyone whom 可以代換成whomever

例2

Anyone whom	this belongs to,	it should be confiscated.
Whomever	this belongs to,	it should be confiscated.

（無論這東西是誰的，都應該被沒收。）

做為belong to的受詞，需要寫whom

3 whosever 指「無論誰的」

whosever為whose＋ever所組成的複合關係代名詞，在關係子句中做主詞或所有格形容詞。

例1

| The decision | , whosever | it is, | is clever. |

（這個決定很聰明，無論是誰做的。）

意思就是 No matter whose decision it is, it is clever. 原來如此！

例2

| Whosever | money | it is, | it should be spent wisely. |

（無論這錢是誰的，都應該明智地花用。）

意思就是 No matter whose money it is, it should be spent wisely. 原來如此！

4 whatever 指「無論什麼；無論何事」

whatever為what＋ever所組成的複合關係代名詞，可以用來取代「先行詞anything＋關係代名詞that」，在關係子句中做主詞或受詞。

關係子句做主詞

例1

Anything	that	he said	is not true.
Whatever		he said	is not true.

（無論他説什麼都不是事實。）

anything that代換成whatever

原來如此！

關係子句做受詞

例2

I will do	anything	that	you want me to do.
I will do	whatever		you want me to do.

（我會做任何你要我做的事。）

★疑問詞what也具有複合關係代名詞的功能，可以用來取代「先行詞the thing(s)＋關係代名詞which」，在關係子句中同樣可做主詞或受詞。

關係子句做主詞

例1

The things	that	you've done	is unforgivable.
What		you've done	is unforgivable.

（你所做過的事是不可原諒的。）

the things that代換成what

原來如此！

關係子句做受詞

例2

I don't care	the things	that	he is doing at all.
I don't care	what		he is doing at all.

（我一點也不在乎他在做些什麼事。）

原來如此！

the things that代換成what

5 whichever 指「無論哪一個」

whichever為which＋ever所組成的複合關係代名詞，可以用來取代「先行詞any one＋關係代名詞that」，可在關係子句中做主詞或受詞。

例1

My budget for a car
is very limited.
關係子句做主詞
（我買車的預算非常有限。）

Any one	that	is the cheapest	is my top choice.
Whichever		is the cheapest	is my top choice.

（無論哪一台，最便宜的就是我的首選。）

原來如此！

Anyone that代換成whichever

例2

I have many evening dresses.
（我有很多晚禮服。）

You can borrow	any one	that	you like.
You can borrow	whichever		you like.

（無論你喜歡哪一件都可以跟我借。）

anyone that代換成whichever

6 wherever 指「無論何處」

wherever為where+ever所組成的複合關係代名詞，可以用來取代「先行詞any place及關係代名詞that，在關係子句中做主詞、受詞或副詞用。

例1

Any place	that	you go,	I will follow.
Wherever		you go,	I will follow.

（無論你到何處，我都相隨。）

any place that代換成wherever

例2

Please put this back to	any place	that	it belongs to.
Please put this back to	wherever		it belongs to.

（請把這個放回它所屬的地方。）

本來是No matter where the book belongs to, please put it back.的意思。

★疑問詞where也具有複合關係代名詞的功能，可以用來取代「先行詞the place ＋關係代名詞which」。

例 • **Where** there is a will, there's a way. （有志者，事竟成。）
　 • **Where** there's life, there's hope. （活者就有希望。）

可以用where代替Wherever

Tips
重點筆記

★關係代名詞which除了取代先行詞，也可以取代一整個句子。

例1 **He cheated in the exam,** (which) makes his teacher very angry.
（他考試作弊，這件事讓他的老師非常生氣。）

which也可以代替逗號整個子句的內容。

請注意！

例2 **The elevator was out of order,** (which) means I had to take the stairs.
（電梯故障了，這表示我得爬樓梯。）

which後面的子句式補充說明。

請注意！

用複合關係代名詞重寫句子

1. Anyone who stops learning is old.

   _____

   _____

2. Any place that he hides, I will find him.

   _____

   _____

3. I'm fine with any one that you choose.

   _____

   _____

4. I'm thankful for anything that you did for me.

   _____

   _____

5. Anyone that solved this math question must be a genius.

   _____

   _____

ANSWER

1. Whoever stops learning is old.
2. Wherever he hides, I will find him.
3. I'm fine with whichever you choose.
4. I'm thankful for whatever you did for me.
5. Whoever solved this math question must be a genius.

Lesson 1
Lesson 2
Lesson 3
Lesson 4
Lesson 5
Lesson 6
Lesson 7
Lesson 8
Lesson 9
Lesson 10

Lesson 3 文法總複習

A 選擇

1. (　) Give the money to _____ needs it.
   A. whoever　　　　　　　B. whomever
   C. people　　　　　　　　D. those

2. (　) Do you know _____ he's always late?
   A. where　　　　　　　　B. when
   C. why　　　　　　　　　D. which

3. (　) The house _____ is built next to the shopping center belongs to my grandfather.
   A. whichever　　　　　　B. where
   C. whosever　　　　　　 D. which

4. (　) This is the year _____ I will become a college student.
   A. which　　　　　　　　B. when
   C. how　　　　　　　　　D. whenever

5. (　) Family is the people who will always stand by you _____ you need support.
   A. whoever　　　　　　　B. wherever
   C. whenever　　　　　　 D. whomever

6. (　) The bike _____ the wheels are broken is mine.
   A. that　　　　　　　　　B. of which
   C. whose　　　　　　　　D. which

7. (　) The man _____ I trusted so much cheated on me.
   A. whom　　　　　　　　B. whomever
   C. what　　　　　　　　　D. whosever

8. (　) I have many shortcomings, _____ is lack of confidence.
   A. which
   B. that
   C. whichever
   D. one of which

9. (　) They looked up in the sky, _____ the stars were shining like little diamonds.
   A. where
   B. which
   C. wherever
   D. about whom

10. (　) I am returning to the town _____ I was born and raised.
   A. which
   B. which in
   C. in which
   D. whichever

B 配合題：為句子選出最適當的關係代名詞

A. whatever　　B. whomever　　C. whosever
D. wherever　　E. whoever

1. _____ said that money can't buy anything didn't know where to go shopping.

2. Do _____ makes you feel comfortable.

3. The puppy followed me _____ I went, so I took it home.

4. _____ you guys are talking about must be a terrible person.

5. _____ car it is, return it immediately.

ANSWER

A. 選擇

1. A　2. C　3. D　4. B　5. C　6. B　7. A　8. D　9. A　10. C

B. 配合題：為句子選出最適當的關係代名詞

1. E　2. A　3. D　4. B　5. C

Lesson 4

疑問句構

Lesson 4

「那就是命運的安排，不是嗎？」
This is destiny, isn't it?

疑問句構

疑問句是用來提出疑問的句型，有「一般疑問句」、「附加問句」以及「間接問句」等三種句型。

一般疑問句可以分為「助動詞疑問句」及「疑問詞疑問句」；附加問句則是接在直述句後，以反問的方式提出疑問；間接問句是將一般疑問句轉做名詞子句，放在直述句中做受詞，間接提出問句，以便讓語氣顯得更為委婉或客氣。

 一般疑問句

1 助動詞疑問句

助動詞疑問句亦可稱為yes/no疑問句，凡以助動詞（含be動詞）為首的疑問句，回答通常是yes或no。

例1

（你期待聖誕節嗎？）

	Are	**you**	looking forward to Christmas?
Yes,	I	am.	

（是的，我很期待。）

問句中的 Are you，變成答句中的 I am 了！

原來如此！

例2

（你不知道賣酒給未成年人是犯法的嗎？）

	Don't	you	know that selling alcohol to minors is against the law?
No,	I	don't.	

（不，我不知道。）

問句中的 Don't you，變成答句中的 I don't 了！

原來如此！

例3

（你們知道布魯克林先生要退休了嗎？）

	Have	you	heard about Mr. Brooklyn's retirement?
Yes,	we **all**	have.	

（有，我們都聽說了。）

問句中的 Have you，變成答句中的We (all) have 了！

原來如此！

文法練習站 ❶

將下列句子改為疑問句

1. Mr. Morgan has retired.

   _____

2. The police will take care of this.

   _____

3. He has some questions for you.

_____

4. Many people were killed in the tsunami.

_____

5. They should have finished their homework before dinner.

_____

ANSWER

1. Has Mr. Morgan retired?
2. Will the police take care of this?
3. Does he have any questions for you?
4. Were many people killed in the tsunami?
5. Should they have finished their homework before dinner?

2 疑問詞疑問句

疑問詞，也稱作疑問代名詞，是用來詢問「具體」答案的詞類。常用的疑問詞如下：

what	問「事物」	where	問「地點、方向」
who	問「身份」	when	問「時間」
why	問「原因」	how	問「方法」

以疑問詞為句首的疑問句，不以yes / no回答，而是必須針對疑問詞的性質提供答案。

例1

what →回答事物

Q **What** did he say to you in the meeting room?
（他跟你在會議室裡面說了什麼？）

A **Nothing** particular. （沒什麼特別的。）

例2

where →回答地點

Q **Where** have you been? Everyone was looking for
you. （你剛剛到哪兒去了？大家都在找你。）

A I went to **the toilet.** （我去廁所了。）

例3

who →回答人物身分

Q **Who** is the man waiting for you at the reception?
（在會客室等你的男子是誰？）

A He's **my fiancé.** （是我未婚夫。）

例4

when →回答時間

Q **When** will the milk expire?
（那牛奶什麼時候到期？）

A **Two days later.** （兩天後。）

例5

why →回答原因

Q **Why** didn't you take the job offer?
（你為什麼不接受那個工作機會？）

A **Because** the pay was not as good as I expected.
（因為薪水不如我預期的好。）

which →回答選項之一

Q **Which** do you prefer, Chinese food or Japanese food? （你比較喜歡哪一種，中國食物或日本食物？）

A I like them **both**. （我兩種都喜歡。）

how →回答方法

Q **How** do you commute between Taipei and Taoyuan?
（你如何通勤於臺北及桃園兩地？）

A I commute **by train**. （我搭火車通勤。）

how →回答方法

Q **How** have you been lately?
（你最近過得如何？）

A **Can't complain.**
（沒什麼好抱怨的。）

how →回答方法

Q **How's** everything going?
（一切進行得還好嗎？）

A Everything's going just **fine**. （一切都很順利。）

Tips

★how後面接不同的形容詞，便可用來詢問不同的事物

☆ how old 問「年齡」
How old can elephants live?
（大象能活到幾歲？）

☆ how many 問「數量」
How many siblings do you have?
（你有幾個兄弟姐妹？）

☆ how many times 問「次數」
How many times do I have to tell you?
（我得告訴你幾次才行？）

☆ how much 問「價格」
How much does this car cost?
（這輛車要多少錢？）

☆ how often 問「頻率」
How often do you hit the gym?
（你多久上健身房一次？）

☆ how long 問「時間」
How long do we have to wait?
（我們得等多久？）

☆ how far 問「距離」
How far is it from here?
（那個地方離這裡有多遠？）

文法練習站 ❷

依劃線部分造原問句

1. The bus runs every 10 minutes.

_____

_____

2. The best way to travel around the city is by MRT.

_____

_____

3. The woman that Mr. Green is talking to is our new English teacher. _____

_____

4. I have to renew my membership by the end of this month.

_____

_____

5. You can buy a ticket using the ticket machine.

_____

_____

附加問句

附加問句是附加在「直述句」後面，用來「向對方確認事實」、「澄清事實「或是「尋求對方認同」的一種簡短問句。

這類問句是以「助動詞＋代名詞」的組合方式，放在直述句後的反問句。所謂反問，也就是在肯定直述句後接否定附加問句，在否定直述句後接肯定附加問句。

重點筆記

★形成附加問句的步驟及重點：

Step 1 ➡️ 判斷直述句——肯定句接否定附加問句；否定句接肯定附加問句。

Step 2 ➡️ 附加問句的主詞——要將直述句的主詞換成代名詞

Step 3 ➡️ 附加問句的be動詞或助動詞——要與直述句相同，且時態需一致。

Step 4 ➡️ 否定附加問句的助動詞與not要縮寫，如doesn't。

☆ am not無法縮寫，因此附加問句要用am I not或是aren't I。

原來如此！

前肯定→後否定；前否定→後肯定

1 一般直述句的附加問句

【肯定直述句＋否定附加問句】

| Step 1 ➡ 肯定改否定 | Step 2 ➡ 主詞改為代名詞 |

例1

Jenny and Amy are best friends, aren't they?

（Jenny和Amy是最好的朋友，不是嗎？）

Step 1 ➡ 原句**are**肯定→附加問句**aren't** 否定。

Step 2 ➡ 原句主詞**Jenny and Amy**→附加問句改為代名詞**they**。

例2

Marie has three daughters, doesn't she?

（Marie有三個女兒，不是嗎？）

Step 1 ➡ 原句**has**肯定→附加問句**doesn't** 否定。

Step 2 ➡ 原句主詞**Mary**→附加問句改為代名詞**she**。

例3

Peter will join us for dinner, won't he?

（Peter會跟我們一起吃晚餐，不是嗎？）

Step 1 ➡ 原句**will**肯定→附加問句**won't** 否定。

Step 2 ➡ 原句主詞**Peter**→附加問句改為代名詞**he**。

例4

They have had lunch already, haven't they?

（他們已經吃過午餐了，不是嗎？）

Step 1 ➡ 原句**have**肯定→附加問句**haven't** 否定。

Step 2 ➡ 原句主詞**they**→附加問句仍為代名詞**they**。

【否定直述句＋肯定附加問句】

Step 1 ⟹ 否定改肯定	**Step 2** ⟹ 主詞改為代名詞

例1

I am not the only person that got laid off, **am I**?

（我不是唯一被裁員的人，對吧？）

Step 1 ⟹ 原句be動詞**am not**否定→附加問句**am**肯定。

Step 2 ⟹ 原句主詞**I**→附加問句仍為**I**

例2

You didn't do it on purpose, **did you**?

（你不是故意那麼做的，對吧？）

Step 1 ⟹ 原句助動詞**didn't**否定→附加問句**did**肯定。

Step 2 ⟹ 原句主詞**you**→附加問句仍為代名詞**you**」

重點筆記

★ 直述中若含有否定意味的字詞，附加問句就要用肯定式。

例1 Your husband seldom loses his temper, **does he**? （你先生很少發脾氣，不是嗎？）

原句seldom有否定意味→附加問句does肯定」

例2 She has never been to Europe, **has she**?

（她從未去過歐洲，不是嗎？）

原句never有否定意味→附加問句has肯定」

依劃線部分造原問句

寫出下列句子的附加問句

1. They didn't go to the same school, _____?

2. You won't tell anyone about this, _____?

3. James seldom invites friends over for dinner, _____?

4. I am always at your side, _____?

5. You must be kidding, _____?

ANSWER

1.did they	3.does he	5.aren't you
2.will you	4.aren't I	

2 特殊主詞的附加問句

直述句的主詞	附加問句主詞
動名詞（片語）、不定詞（片語）、this、that、everything、something、nothing、anything等	it
these、those、everybody、everyone、nobody、someone、anyone等	they
there	there

例1

Being a fashion designer is your dream, **isn't it**?

（成為一名服裝設計師是你的夢想，不是嗎？）

原句主詞 Being a fashion designer
→附加問句用代名詞 it

原來如此！

例2

Nobody has the right to take a life, **do they**?

（沒有人有權利奪走一個生命，不是嗎？）

原句主詞 nobody
→附加問句用代名詞 they

原來如此！

例3

There is a post office behind the hospital, **isn't there**?

（醫院後面有一間郵局，不是嗎？）

原句用虛主詞 there
→附加問句同樣用 there

原來如此！

文法練習站 ❹

依劃線部分造原問句

寫出下列句子的附加問句

1. Everyone is looking forward to the party, _____?

2. There are many people waiting to be served, _____?

3. Looking after three toddlers can be very tiring, _____?

4. Everything is under control, _____?

5. That is not what she told us, _____?

3 祈使句的附加問句

【一般祈使句】

一般祈使句為省略主詞you的命令句，無論是肯定或否定祈使句，附加問句一律為will you?

例1

祈使句

| Do me a favor | , will you? |

（幫我個忙，好嗎？）

例2

祈使句

| Don't let me down | , will you? |

（不要讓我失望，好嗎？）

原來如此！

原句為否定Don't 開頭，也是用will you喔！

100

Lesson 1
Lesson 2
Lesson 3
Lesson 4
Lesson 5
Lesson 6
Lesson 7
Lesson 8
Lesson 9
Lesson 10

【 Let's祈使句 】

　　Let's 的句型是用來表示「提議」，動作會在未來時間執行，故助動詞用shall；此類祈使句的對象為us，因此附加問句主詞用we。無論是肯定提議或否定提議，附加問句都是肯定式shall we?

例1

| Let's take a break, | shall we? |

（我們休息一下好嗎？）

例2

| Let's not talk about this right now, | shall we? |

（我們現在別談這件事，好嗎？）

原來如此！

原句為否定Let's not 開頭，也是用shall we喔！

文法練習站 ❺

　　寫出下列句子的附加問句

1. Take good care of yourself, ＿＿＿＿＿＿＿?

2. Let's talk about it later, ＿＿＿＿＿＿＿?

3. Don't make me wait too long, ＿＿＿＿＿＿＿?

4. Be nice to your sister, ＿＿＿＿＿＿＿?

5. Let's just ask him for help, ＿＿＿＿＿＿＿?

 間接問句

　　將直接問句併入另一個句子，以間接方式提出問句，即為間接問句。被併入另一個句子的問句，成為主要句子的附屬子句，在主句中為動詞的受詞。直接問句的疑問詞通常就是引導這個附屬子句的連接詞。

　　既然是子句，句型結構就是一般句子的結構，也就是「主詞＋動詞＋……」，而不是問句的「助動詞＋主詞＋動詞＋……」的結構，因此要將直接問句改成間接問句時，要將問句句構倒裝回直述句的句構。

間接問句常用的連接詞	
直接問句形式	間接問句連接詞
be動詞疑問句 / 助動詞疑問句	whether
疑問詞疑問句	what, who, where, how, when, why

1 助動詞（含be動詞）疑問句

　　助動詞（含be動詞）疑問句的回答通常與「是與否」有關，因此改為間接問句時，連接詞用有「是否」含義的whether。

例1

（我不確定。）

| 1. 主要子句→ | I'm not sure. | |
| 2. 間接問句原句→ | | Is Julia qualified to do the job? |

（Julia是否具備做這工作的必要條件？）

Step 1 ➡ 把句2改為直述句構。

請跟著步驟這樣做！

Julia is qualified to do the job.

Step 2 ➡ 把改造過的句2直接加在句1之後，就會變成：

I'm not sure whether Julia is qualified to do the job.

（我不確定Julia是否具備做這工作的必要條件。）

例2

（沒有人知道。）

| 1. 主要子句→ | Nobody knows. | |
| 2. 間接問句原句→ | | Does the woman have any health problems? |

（這女子有任何健康問題嗎？）

Step 1 ➡ 把句2改為直述句構。

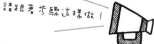

請跟著步驟這樣做！

the woman has any health problems.

Step 2 ➡ 把改造過的句2直接加在句1之後，就會變成：

Nobody knows whether the woman has any health problems.

（沒有人知道這女子是否有任何健康問題。）

沒有助動詞does，動詞要變成第3人稱單數。

完成下列句子的間接問句

1. Has Jennifer returned yet?

   I don't know _____.

2. Is Mr. White available to see me now?

   Can you check for me _____

   _____?

3. Did anyone call me this morning?

   Do you know _____?

4. Was the man still alive?

   Nobody was told _____.

5. Will the ceremony be held as scheduled?

   When will we know _____

   _____?

ANSWER

1. whether Jennifer has returned
2. whether Mr. White is available to see me now
3. whether anyone called me this morning
4. whether the man was still alive
5. whether the ceremony will be held as scheduled

2 疑問詞疑問句

　　直接問句為疑問詞疑問句時，句首的疑問詞就是間接問句的連接詞。連接詞在句子中引導一個名詞子句作為主句中動詞的受詞，因此必須將疑問句句構倒裝回一般直述句句構。

例1

（你記得嗎？）

1. 主要子句→	Do you remember?		
2. 間接問句原句→		What	is our high school teacher's name?

（我們高中老師的名字是什麼？）

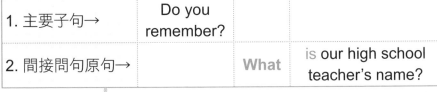

Step 1 ➡ 把句2改為直述句構。

what our high school teacher's name is.
（保留疑問詞what）

Step 2 ➡ 把改造過的句2直接加在句1之後，就會變成：

Do you remember what our high school teacher's name is?

（你記得我們高中老師的名字叫什麼嗎？）

例2

（你知道嗎？）

1. 主要子句→	Do you have any idea?		
2. 間接問句原句→		Where	can the children possibly go?

（孩子們可能會去哪裡？）

Step 1 ➡ 把句2改為直述句構。

where the children can possibly go.
（保留疑問詞where）

Do you have any idea where the children can possibly go?

（你知道孩子們有可能會去哪裡嗎？）

例3

（請告訴我。）

1. 主要子句→	Please tell me.		
2. 間接問句原句→		How	do you deal with difficult customers?

（你如何應付難纏的顧客？）

Step 1 ➡ 把句2改為直述句構。

how you deal with difficult customers.

（去掉助動詞do、保留疑問詞how）

Step 2 ➡ 把改造過的句2直接加在句1之後，就會變成：

Please tell me how you deal with difficult customers.

（請告訴我你是如何應付難纏的顧客。）

★ 當疑問詞本身就是主詞時，間接問句中的子句結構順序不變：

例1

（我一定要知道。）

1. 主要子句→	I must know.	
2. 間接問句原句→		Who did this?

（誰做了這種事？）

➡ 句2不用更動字序，直接加在主要子句之後，就會變成：

who就是主詞

I must know <u>who</u> did this.

（我一定要知道是誰做了這種事。）

例2

（別告訴任何人。）

1. 主要子句→	Don't tell anyone.	
2. 間接問句原句→		What's there inside the box?

（盒子裡有什麼？）

➡ 句2不用更動字序，直接加在主要子句之後，就會變成：

Don't tell anyone <u>what</u> is there inside the box.

（不要告訴任何人盒子裡有什麼。）

what就是主詞

完成下列間接問句

1. What did Mr. Smith say on the phone?

   I'd like to know _____.

2. What is the longest river in the world?

   Does anyone know _____?

3. What is there in your hands?

   Can you show me _____?

4. How does he manage such a large company?

   I have no idea _____.

5. Why is learning English necessary?

   I don't know _____.

ANSWER

1. what Mr. Smith said on the phone.
2. what the longest river in the world is
3. what is there in your hands
4. how he manages such a large company
5. why learning English is necessary

 Tips

 重點筆記

★ 間接問句子句簡化為不定詞 ★

當間接問句的前後子句的主詞為同一人，或主要子句的受詞與附屬子句的主詞為同一人時，子句的「主詞＋助動詞＋動詞」可以簡化為「疑問詞＋不定詞」

例1

（我想知道。）

1. 主要子句→	I'd like to know.	
2. 間接問句原句→		Where can I buy the ticket?

（我可以在哪裡買到票？）

Step 1 → 把句2換成直述句構、保留疑問詞。

請跟著步驟
這樣做！

where **I can buy the ticket.**

Step 2 → 改造過的句2接在句1之後，就會變成：

I'd like to know where **I can buy the ticket.**

Step 3 → 間接問句中的主詞＋助動詞→to動詞，就會變成：

I'd like to know where to buy **the ticket.**

（我想知道哪裡可以買掉票。）

例2

（你應該要教他們的。）

1. 主要子句→	You should have taught them.	
2. 間接問句原句→		How should they do the experiment?

（他們應該怎麼做這個實驗？）

Step 1 → 把句2換成直述句構、保留疑問詞。

請跟著步驟
這樣做！

how **they should do the experiment.**

Step 2 → 改造過的句2接在句1之後，就會變成：

You should have taught them how **they should do the experiment.**

Step 3 ➡ 間接問句中的主詞＋助動詞→to動詞，就會變成：

You should have taught them how to do the experiment.
（你應該教他們怎麼做實驗。）

文法練習站 ❽

將間接問句簡化為不定詞

1. Do you know what you must do next?

_____

2. I didn't tell my husband where he could find his socks.

_____

3. I don't know how I should take care of a little baby.

_____

4. Could you let me know whom I should talk to?

_____

5. I would be appreciated if you could tell me how I can get there.

_____

ANSWER

1. Do you know what to do next?
2. I didn't tell my husband where to find his socks.
3. I don't know how to take care of a little baby.
4. Could you let me know whom to talk to?
5. I would be appreciated if you could tell me how to get there.

Lesson 1

Lesson 2

Lesson 3

Lesson 4

Lesson 5

Lesson 6

Lesson 7

Lesson 8

Lesson 9

Lesson 10

Lesson 4

文法總複習

A 選擇

1. (　) Dad must be very upset, _____?
   A. mustn't Dad
   B. is Dad
   C. isn't he
   D. must he

2. (　) You haven't met my boyfriend, John, _____?
   A. did you
   B. have you
   C. don't you
   D. has he

3. (　) Put this on my desk, _____?
   A. shall we
   B. won't you
   C. is it
   D. will you

4. (　) Let's leave him alone, _____?
   A. shall we
   B. should we
   C. will you
   D. do you

5. (　) We have little rice to eat, _____?
   A. don't we
   B. haven't we
   C. do we
   D. have we

6. (　) There isn't anything for me to do, _____?
   A. is it　　B. is there　　C. isn't it　　D. isn't there

7. (　) That's the hospital where I was born, _____?
   A. isn't it　　B. isn't that　　C. wasn't it　　D. was that

8. (　) I think they have already gone, _____?
   A. aren't they
   B. haven't they
   C. don't I
   D. didn't they

9. (　) Being a mom isn't an easy task, _____?
   A. isn't she　　B. does it　　C. is it　　D. is she

B 寫出間接問句

1. Do you want to go to the movies with me?
   I'm wondering _____

   _____.

2. Can I reschedule my appointment with Dr. Cooper?
   I'd like to know _____

   _____?

3. Are they allowed to smoke here?
   I'm not sure _____

   _____.

4. What are the requirements for this position?
   Do you happen to know _____

   _____?

5. Why can't I bring food into the cinema?
   I don't know _____

   _____.

6. When will the restaurant reopen for business?
   She must know _____

   _____.

7. Did you reserve a hotel room for the business trip?
   The manager asked me _____

   _____.

8. Who will join the contest on behalf of our school?
   The principal announced _____

   _____.

9. What gift should we send them as a token of gratitude?
   Let's discuss _____
   _____.

10. Where will they go for their honeymoon?
    I tried to find out _____
    _____.

11. Which form am I supposed to fill in?
    Please tell me _____
    _____.

12. Had she dealt with the case?
    The boss wanted to know _____
    _____.

ANSWER

A. 選擇

1. C　2. B　3. D　4. A　5. C　6. B　7. A　8. B　9. C

B. 寫出間接問句

1. whether you want to go to the movies with me
2. whether I can reschedule my appointment with Dr. Cooper
3. whether they are allowed to smoke here.
4. what the requirements for this position are
5. why I can't bring food into the cinema
6. when the restaurant will reopen for business
7. whether you reserved a hotel room for the business trip.
8. who will join the contest on behalf of our school.
9. what gift we should send them as a token of gratitude.
10. where they will go for their honeymoon.
11. which form I am supposed to fill in.
12. whether she had dealt with the case.

Lesson 5

強調語氣 I——
分裂句

"「就是她，我一眼就看到的人。」

It is her that I fell in love
with at the first sight.

強調語氣 I ——分裂句

　　將一個完整的句子分裂成兩個子句，即所謂的「分裂句」。分裂句的目的在將句子的資訊拆成兩個部分：「已知資訊」及「未知資訊」。我們會在説話時，利用分裂句將對方已經知道的事情（已知資訊）與對方還不知道的事情（未知資訊）產生關連，藉此來強調新資訊。

　　英文的分裂句可分為 It-分裂句和 Wh-分裂句。這兩種句型都是把想要傳達給對方的重要資訊放在強調位置，其他的部分全都放在that之後，即可達到加強語氣的目的。

It-分裂句

句構：It is / was＋新資訊＋that 舊資訊

例1　　　　　　　　　（舊資訊→我正在找某物。）

| 1. 舊資訊→ | I am looking for | something. |
| 2. 新資訊→ | I am looking for | a black puppy. |

（新資訊→我正在找一隻黑色的小狗狗。）

 Step 1 ➡ 找出強調的訊息 a black puppy。

請跟著步驟
這樣做！

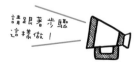

116

Step 2 強調的訊息放在 **It is** 和 **that** 的中間。

Step 3 句1 舊資訊接在 **that** 的後面，就會變成：

It is a black puppy that I am looking for.
（我正在找的是一隻黑色的小狗狗。）

原來你在找的是黑色的小狗狗！

例2

（舊資訊→這班火車要開往某處。）

1. 舊資訊→	This train is bound for	somewhere.
2. 新資訊→	This train is bound for	Shanghai.

（新資訊→這班火車要開往上海。）

Step 1 找出強調的訊息 Shanghai。

請跟著步驟這樣做！

Step 2 強調的訊息放在 **It is** 和 **that** 的中間。

Step 3 句1 舊資訊接在 **that** 的後面，就會變成：

It is Shanghai that this train is bound for.
（這班火車所要前往的地點是上海。）

that 前面可以是「名詞」、「代名詞」、「副詞」、「片語」或是「副詞子句」，以強調不同的重點。

原來如此！

1▸ 強調主詞

例1

It was	I	that	gave birth to you.
強調句構	強調的資訊	強調句構	舊資訊

（是我把你生下來的。）

生下你的是我！不是別人！

例2

But it was	Aunt Lily	that	raised me up.
強調句構	強調的資訊	強調句構	舊資訊

（但是把我養大的卻是Lily阿姨。）

養大我的是Lily阿姨！不是你！

2▸ 強調受詞

例1

It is	a white watch	that	I am looking for.
強調句構	強調的資訊	強調句構	舊資訊

（我正在找的是一只白色的手錶。）

原來你在找的是一只白色的手錶！

例2

It is	your brother	that	I love.
強調句構	強調的資訊	強調句構	舊資訊

（我所愛的人是你的哥哥。）

原來你愛的人是我的哥哥！

3 強調副詞

例1

It was	yesterday	that	the party was held.
強調句構	強調的資訊	強調句構	舊資訊

（派對舉行的時間是昨天。）

原來是昨天！（我以為是今天！）

例2

It is	in September	that	we're going to get married.
強調句構	強調的資訊	強調句構	舊資訊

（我們是要在九月結婚。）

原來是在九月！（我還以為更早！）

例3

It is	in the city hall	that	the inauguration will take place.
強調句構	強調的資訊	強調句構	舊資訊

（就職典禮舉辦的地方將是在市政廳。）

原來是在市政廳！（我還以為在別的地方！）

例4

It was	under the bed	that	the man hid his weapon.
強調句構	強調的資訊	強調句構	舊資訊

（男子藏匿武器的地方就是在床下。）

原來是在床下！（之前找錯地方了！）

☆ 強調的句型，有要聽話者特別注意被強調的資訊、不要弄錯了的意味在。

將要強調的畫線部分改成it分裂句

1. We are talking about <u>our history teacher</u>.

   _____

   _____

2. I started learning swimming <u>during the summer vacation</u>.

   _____

   _____

3. He is going to be a college student <u>in the coming September</u>.

   _____

   _____

4. The prince is going to marry <u>a peasant girl</u>.

   _____

   _____

5. My husband and I went to <u>Hawaii</u> for our honeymoon trip.

   _____

   _____

ANSWER

1. It is our history teacher that we're talking about.
2. It was during that summer vacation that I started learning swimming.
3. It is in the coming September that he is going to be a college student.
4. It is a peasant girl that the prince is going to marry.
5. It is Hawaii that my husband and I went for our honeymoon trip.

重點筆記

★that的省略★

當It-分裂句使用在口語或非正式場合時，作為子句中受詞的that通常省略不用。

例1

It is	**your brother**	**(that)**	**we're talking about.**
強調句構	強調的資訊	強調句構	舊資訊

（我們正在談論你的哥哥。）

原本的句子是 We're talking about your brother. 強調的 your brother 是受詞，換成強調句型後，that可省略。
原來如此！

例2

It is	**my car**	**(that)**	**you're driving.**
強調句構	強調的資訊	強調句構	舊資訊

（你現在開的可是我的車。）

原本的句子是 You're driving my car. 強調的 my car 是受詞，換成強調句型後，that可省略。
原來如此！

★以who代替that★

當It-分裂句強調的是「人」，可以用 who 來代替 that。在口語或非正式場合，作為子句中受詞的whom可省略。

121

例1

It is	Frank	(whom / that)	my sister is dating.
強調句構	強調的資訊	強調句構	舊資訊

（我妹妹正在交往的人就是Frank。）

原本的句子是My sister is dating Frank. 強調的 Frank 是受詞，換成強調句型後，whom / that 可省略。」

原來如此！

例2

It was	Vincent	(whom / that)	Mr. Lin fired last week.
強調句構	強調的資訊	強調句構	舊資訊

（林先生上星期開除的人就是Vincent。）

原本的句子是Mr. Lin fired Vincent last week. 強調的 Vincent 是受詞，換成強調句型後，whom / that 可省略。

原來如此！

文法練習站 ❷

that可以省略的在空格內打X，不可省略的則寫出that或who

1. I was angry, because it was my sister _____ the boys were making fun of.

2. It was Mr. Lee _____ showed us around the city.

3. It is people who trust you _____ you're lying to.

4. It is Jennifer _____ borrowed the book from me.

5. It is colon cancer _____ David was diagnosed with.

ANSWER

1. X   2. that   3. X   4. that / who   5. X

重點筆記

★否定結構的分裂句★

例1

It wasn't	I	that	revealed your secret to others.
否定強調句構	強調的資訊	強調句構	舊資訊

（把你的秘密洩漏給別人的人並不是我。）

Someone revealed your secret, but it wasn't me. 有人洩漏你的祕密，但不是我喔！

例2

It wasn't	money	that	caused problems in our relationship.
否定強調句構	強調的資訊	強調句構	舊資訊

（造成我們關係出現問題的原因並不是金錢。）

Something caused problems in our relationship, but it wasn't money. 有些事情造成我們關係出現問題，但不是錢的問題！

★若分裂句中所強調的人或事物是「複數」，that子句的動詞必須用複數動詞，但主句的主詞為虛主詞 it，be動詞仍維持單數 is或 was。

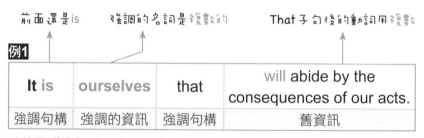

例1

It is	ourselves	that	will abide by the consequences of our acts.
強調句構	強調的資訊	強調句構	舊資訊

（將承受我們的行為後果的人正是我們自己。）

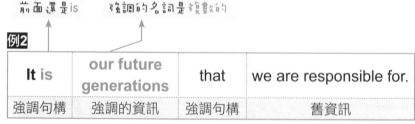

例2

It is	our future generations	that	we are responsible for.
強調句構	強調的資訊	強調句構	舊資訊

（我們所要負責的對象正是我們的後代子孫。）

文法練習站 ❸

將下列分裂句改為否定式

1. It was Linda that wanted a divorce.

_____

124

2. It is a boy that the couple is expecting.

_____

3. It was on the Valentine's Day that George proposed to Anita.

_____

4. It was laziness that caused his failure.

_____

5. It was an earthquake that destroyed this village.

_____

ANSWER

1. It wasn't Linda that wanted a divorce.
2. It isn't a boy that the couple is expecting.
3. It wasn't on the Valentine's Day that George proposed to Anita.
4. It wasn't laziness that caused his failure.
5. It wasn't an earthquake that destroyed this village.

Wh-分裂句

句構：Wh-子句＋is / was ＋新資訊

　　Wh-分裂句又稱為「準分裂句」，常用來引導 Wh-分裂句的疑問代名詞有what、why、where、how 等。Wh-子句中的資訊是已經知道的舊資訊，整個子句視為單數名詞，故be動詞恆為is；be動詞後的補語，就是所要強調的新資訊。

例1

（舊資訊→你現在需要某樣東西。）

1. 舊資訊→	You need	something	now.
2. 新資訊→	You need	a decent job and a steady income.	

（新資訊→你需要一份像樣的工作和一份穩定的收入。）

Step 1 ⟶ 找出強調的訊息 **a decent job and steady income**。

Step 2 ⟶ 判斷強調的訊息是事物，疑問詞用 **What**。

Step 3 ⟶ 句1 舊資訊接在 **What** 的後面，就會變成：

What	you need now	is	a decent job and a steady income.
疑問詞	舊資訊	be動詞	新資訊／強調的資訊

（你現在所需要的就是一份像樣的工作和一份穩定的收入。）

例2

（舊資訊→龍滅絕了。）

1. 舊資訊→		Dinosaurs went extinct.	
2. 新資訊→	The reason	(why dinosaurs went extinct)	is still mysterious.

（新資訊→原因仍然是個謎。）

Step 1 ⟶ 找出強調的訊息 **is still mysterious**。

Step 2 ⟶ 判斷強調的訊息是事物，疑問詞用 **Why**。

Step 3 ⟶ 句1 舊資訊接在 **Why** 的後面，就會變成：

Why	dinosaurs went extinct	is	still mysterious.
疑問詞	舊資訊	be動詞	新資訊／強調的資訊

（恐龍滅絕的原因至今仍是個謎。）

例3　　　　　　　　（舊資訊→她把錢藏在某個地方。）

		She hid the money	somewhere.
1. 舊資訊→		She hid the money	somewhere.
2. 新資訊→	It (the place)	(where she hid the money)	is known to few people

（新資訊→沒什麼人知道。）

Step 1 ⟶ 找出強調的訊息 is unknown。

請跟著步驟
這樣做！

Step 2 ⟶ 判斷強調的訊息是事物，疑問詞用 **Where**。

Step 3 ⟶ 句1 舊資訊接在 **Where** 的後面，就會變成：

Where	she hid the money	is	known to few people.
疑問詞	舊資訊	be動詞	新資訊／強調的資訊

（她藏錢的地方並沒有什麼人知道。）

文法練習站 ❹

用wh-分裂句合併句子

1. He escaped from the cage. The way is incredible.

_____

2. I'm going to say something now. It is very important.

_____

3. The man was killed. The reason is under investigation.

_____

4. We have achieved something. It is beyond our widest dreams.

_____

5. They are going to have their wedding at a place. It is going to surprise you.

_____

ANSWER

1. How he escaped from the cage is incredible.
2. What I am going to say now is very important.
3. Why the man was killed is under investigation.
4. What we have achieved is beyond our wildest dreams.
5. Where they're going to have their wedding is going to surprise you.

 Tips ——————————— 重點筆記

★ wh-分裂句的be動詞後的補語若為不定詞片語，可以省略to，無論主句時態為何，be動詞後面都是接「原形動詞」。

現在式is　　　　原形動詞

例1

What	you need to do now	is	(to) finish your homework.
疑問詞	舊資訊	be動詞	新資訊／強調的資訊

（你現在需要做的事情就是把回家作業完成。）

過去式was　　　　原形動詞

例1

What	he did right after he arrived	was	(to) give his mother a call.
疑問詞	舊資訊	be動詞	新資訊／強調的資訊

（他抵達後立刻做的事，就是打電話給媽媽。）

文法練習站 ❺

將劃線部分以wh-分裂句強調

1. He asked me to reserve a table at the Italian restaurant.

　_____

2. I was told to return this to the store.

　_____

3. We can only wait for the results now.

　_____

4. She went for a walk after dinner.

　_____

5. We must separate the garbage correctly first.

　_____

ANSWER

1. What he asked me to do is (to) reserve a table at the restaurant.
2. What I was told to do is to return this to the store.
3. What we can only do now is to wait for the results.
4. What she did after dinner was (to) go for a walk.
5. What we must do first is (to) separate the garbage correctly.

文法總複習

A 選擇

1. (　) It is this car _____ cost me ten thousand dollars to repair.
   A. which
   B. what
   C. where
   D. that

2. (　) It _____ his attitude that irritated me.
   A. was
   B. be
   C. being
   D. will be

3. (　) _____ interests me most is Logan's adventure in Tahiti.
   A. Which
   B. That
   C. What
   D. Who

4. (　) _____ I solved the problem is not important.
   A. What
   B. How
   C. Who
   D. Which

5. (　) It is my mother _____ encourages me to take the opportunity.
   A. who
   B. X
   C. which
   D. whom

6. (　) It _____ these people that forced Jamie to quit his job.
   A. are
   B. was
   C. will be
   D. were

7. (　) What _____ me most is the mischievous gossip.
   A. bothering
   B. bother
   C. brother
   D. bothers

B 翻譯下列句子

1. 總是抱怨自己很忙的人都是懶惰的人。

_____

2. 就在1973年，世界上第一支手機被發明了。

_____

3. 我們會成為好朋友，是因為我們有很多共通點。

_____

_____

4. 應該對這個錯誤負起責任的人是你。

_____

_____

5. 當我需要幫助時，對我伸出援手的人就是James。

_____

6. 他為何自殺，至今仍是個謎團。

_____

_____

7. 他現在最需要的就是我們的支持。

_____

_____

8. 最讓我生氣的就是他厚顏無恥的態度。(irritate / impudent)

_____

_____

ANSWER

A. 選擇

1. D 2. A 3. C 4. B 5. A 6. B 7. D

B. 翻譯下列句子

1. It is lazy people that always complain about being busy.
2. It was in 1973 that the first cellphone in the world was invented.
3. It is because we have a lot in common that we became good friends.
4. It is you that should be the responsible for this mistake.
5. It is James that helped me when I was in need.
6. Why he committed suicide is still a mystery.
7. What he needs most right now is our support.
8. What irritates me most is his impudent attitude.

Lesson 6

強調語氣 II──
倒裝句構

Lesson 6

「若沒遇見她，我人生就是黑白的！」

Had I not met her, I would be tired of my life!

強調語氣Ⅱ——倒裝句構

英文句型中的倒裝句構，是藉由倒裝句子中的字序來加強語氣，達到強調句子中某些元素的目的。

本篇將逐一詳細介紹英文句型中的五大倒裝句構，即「否定倒裝句構」、「only倒裝句構」、「so/such倒裝句構」、「地方副詞倒裝句構」以及「假設倒裝句構」。

否定倒裝句構

否定倒裝句構就是將否定句中具否定含義的副詞（包括片語及子句）移到句首，以強調句子的否定語氣。

否定副詞	never, seldom, hardly, little等
否定副詞片語	under no circumstances, by no means等
否定副詞子句	not until ...

①▶ be動詞的否定倒裝：

否定副詞、否定副詞片語、否定副詞子句移到句首後，be動詞與主詞倒裝。

例1

倒裝前

Astronomy	is	never	boring.
主詞	Be動詞	否定副詞	主詞補語（形容詞）

倒裝後

Never	is	Astronomy	boring.
否定副詞	動詞	主詞	主詞補語（形容詞）

（天文學永遠不會讓人感到無聊。）

否定副詞 never 往前移！主詞 Astronomy 往後移！ 原來如此！

例2

倒裝前

They	are	by no means	my biological parents.
主詞	Be動詞	否定副詞	主詞補語（名詞片語）

倒裝後

By no means	are	they	my biological parents.
否定副詞	Be動詞	主詞	主詞補語（形容詞）

（他們絕不可能是我的親生父母。）

否定副詞片語 by no means 往前移！主詞 they 往後移！ 原來如此！

例3

倒裝前

He	was	not	aware of the problem	until now.
主詞	Be動詞	否定副詞	主詞補語（形容詞）	否定副詞

倒裝後

Not until now	was	he	aware of the problem.
否定副詞	Be動詞	主詞	主詞補語（形容詞）

（一直到現在他才意識到出了問題。）

否定副詞片語 not...until now 往前移！主詞 he 往後移！

原來如此！

2 助動詞的否定倒裝：

　　否定副詞、否定副詞片語、否定副詞子句移到句首後，助動詞與主詞倒裝。

例1

倒裝前

I	have	never	seen this man before.
主詞	助動詞	否定副詞	主要動詞

倒裝後

Never	have	I	seen this man before.
否定副詞	助動詞	主詞	主要動詞

（我從來沒有見過這個男人。）

否定副詞 never 和助動詞 have 往前移！主詞 I 往後移！

原來如此！

例2

倒裝前

You	should	trust strangers	under no circumstances.
主詞	助動詞	主要動詞	否定副詞片語

倒裝後

Under no circumstances	should	you	trust strangers.
否定副詞	助動詞	主詞	主要動詞

（在任何情況下，你都不應該相信陌生人。）

否定副詞片語 under no circumstances 和助動詞 should 往前移！主詞 you 往後移！

原來如此！

例3

倒裝前

He	did	not	realize his mistake	until it caused damage.
主詞	助動詞	否定詞	主要動詞	否定副詞子句

倒裝後

Not	until it caused damage	did	he	realize his mistake.
否定詞	否定副詞子句	助動詞	主詞	主要動詞

（一直到造成損害，他才意識到失誤。）

否定副詞子句 not、until it caused damage 和助動詞 did 往前移！主詞 he 往後移！

原來如此！

3 一般動詞的否定倒裝：

配合主詞及時態加入助動詞do, does或did。將否定副詞、否定副詞片語、否定副詞子句移到句首之後，再將助動詞與主詞倒裝。

例1

倒裝前

She	(does)	never	lets me down.
主詞	助動詞	否定副詞	主要動詞

倒裝後

Never	does	she	let me down.
否定副詞	助動詞	主詞	主要動詞

（她從不讓我失望。）

> 肯定句倒裝後，加上助動詞 does，所以she之後的 let 不用加s！
>
> 原來如此！

例2

倒裝前

My parents	(do)	always support me	without condition.
主詞	助動詞	主要動詞	否定副詞片語

倒裝後

Without condition	do	my parents	always support me.
否定副詞片語	助動詞	主詞	主要動詞

（我的爸媽總是無條件地支持我。）

> 否定副詞片語往前移！加上助動詞，再接主詞。
>
> 原來如此！

文法練習站 ❶

將下列句子以倒裝句強調

1. The house collapsed without any warning.

   _____

2. We can hardly understand what he says.

   _____

3. She will forgive you under no circumstances.

   _____

4. The man didn't admit that he was guilty until the police found the evidence.

   _____

5. Helen is by no means a thrifty housekeeper.

   _____

ANSWER

1. Without any warning did the house collapsed.
2. Hardly can we understand what he says.
3. Under no circumstances will she forgive you.
4. Not until the police found the evidence did the man admit that he was guilty.
5. By no means is Helen a thrifty housekeeper.

only倒裝句構

　　only倒裝句構，就是將句子中的only副詞子句移到句首，以強調句子的否定語氣。將only子句移到句首後，be動詞/助動詞與主詞倒裝。

例1

倒裝前

The baby	is	quiet	only when he is with his mother.
主詞	be動詞	主詞補語（形容詞）	only副詞子句

倒裝後

Only when he is with his mother.	is	the baby	quiet.
only副詞子句	be動詞	主詞	主詞補語（形容詞）

（只有跟媽媽在一起的時候，寶寶才安靜下來。）

only副詞子句往前移！主詞往後移！

原來如此！

例2

倒裝前

I	will	proceed with my speech	only when you quiet down.
主詞	助動詞	句子主要動詞	only副詞子句

倒裝後

Only when you quiet down	will	I	proceed with my speech.
only副詞子句	助動詞	主詞	句子主要動詞

（只有當你們安靜下來，我才會繼續進行演說。）

only副詞子句往前移！且助動詞也往前移！
主詞往後移！

原來如此！

例3

倒裝前

He	(did)	succeeded	only because he never quit.
主詞	助動詞	句子主要動詞	only副詞子句

倒裝後

Only because he never quit	did	he	succeed.
only副詞子句	助動詞	主詞	句子主要動詞

（他會成功，就是因為他永不言棄。）

only副詞子句往前移！加入助動詞did！主詞往後移！

原來如此！

Tips

★ not only ... but also ...的倒裝 ★

將not only ... but also ...的句型做倒裝時，not only子句的be動詞/助動詞與主詞倒裝，but also的句子不須倒裝，但是要加上代名詞，並把also移到be動詞/助動詞後，或直接省略不用。

重點筆記

例1

倒裝前

My boss	is	not only	stubborn	but also	unreasonable.
主詞	Be動詞	倒裝句型	形容詞1	倒裝句型	形容詞2

141

Step 1 ➞ **not only** 移至句首、主詞 **my boss** 往後移。

Step 2 ➞ **but** 之前加上逗號。

Step 3 ➞ **but** 和 **also** 中間加上「代名詞＋**be**動詞」，就會變成：

倒裝後

Not only	is	my boss	stubborn,	but	he is	also	unreasonable.
倒裝句型	Be動詞	主詞	形容詞1	倒裝句型	主詞	倒裝句型	形容詞2

（我老闆不僅頑固，而且還蠻不講理。）

not only...but also... 前後要接相同詞性的字喔！

例2

We	will	not only	visit Lady Liberty,
主詞	助動詞	句型	主要動詞1

but also	walk up to the crown and look down the whole New York City.
句型	主要動詞2

Step 1 ➞ **not only** 移至句首、主 **we** 往後移。

Step 2 ➞ **but** 之前加上逗號。

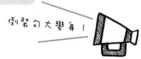

Step 3 ➡ **but** 和 **also** 中間加上代名詞+助動詞 **will**，就會變成：

倒裝後

Not only	will	we	visit Lady Liberty,	but	we will
句型	助動詞	主詞	主要動詞1	句型	主詞+助動詞

also	walk up to the crown and look down the whole New York City.
句型	主要動詞2

（我們不僅會參觀自由女神像，還會爬到王冠俯瞰整個紐約市。）

not only...but also... 前後接的都是動詞！　原來如此！

例3

He	(did)	not only	caught the dogs
主詞	助動詞	倒裝句型	主要動詞1

but also	abused them.
倒裝句型	主要動詞2

倒裝句大變身！

Step 1 ➡ **not only** 移至句首、主詞 **he** 往後移，加上助動詞 **did**。

Step 2 ➡ **but** 之前加上逗號。

Step 3 ➡ **but** 和 **also** 中間加上代名詞，就會變成：

倒裝後

Not only	did	he	catch the dogs
主詞	助動詞	主詞	主要動詞1

but	he	also	abused them.
倒裝句型	主詞	倒裝句型	主要動詞2

（他不僅抓狗，還虐待它們。）

後半段的 he also abused them 肯定句，不用像前半句一樣加上且助動詞喔！

原來如此！

文法練習站 ❷

以倒裝句改寫下列句子

1. The earthquake not only destroyed the village, but also took 30 people's lives.

   _____

   _____

2. The boy only behaves himself when his parents are around.

   _____

3. You will only pass the finals by studying hard.

   _____

4. He can only quit alcohol by seeking treatment.

   _____

5. I come here not only to see you but also to tell you some good news.

   _____

   _____

ANSWER

1. Not only did the earthquake destroy the village, but it also took 30 people's lives.
2. Only when his parents are around does the boy behave himself.
3. Only by studying hard will you pass the finals.
4. Only by seeking treatment can he quit alcohol.
5. Not only do I come here to see you, but I come here to tell you some good news

 so/such倒裝句構

so ... that ...與such ... that...的句型的倒裝方式與否定倒裝句構相同，將so或such移到句首，並將主詞與be動詞／助動詞倒裝即可。後面的that子句則不受倒裝影響。

1 so ... that ... 倒裝：

配合主詞及時態加入助動詞do, does或did。將否定副詞、否定副詞片語、否定副詞子句移到句首之後，再將助動詞與主詞倒裝。

例1

倒裝前

Alex	is	so	**easygoing**	**that** he gets along with almost everyone.
主詞	Be動詞	句型	形容詞	that子句

Step 1 ➡ So+形容詞 **easygoing** 移至句首。

Step 2 ➡ 主詞 **Alex** 移至 **be** 動詞後。

倒裝句大變身！

Step 3 ➡ that子句不動，就會變成：

倒裝後

So	**easygoing**	**is**	Alex	**that** he gets along with almost everyone.
句型	形容詞	Be動詞	主詞	that子句

（Alex非常隨和，幾乎跟每個人都處得很好。）

例2

倒裝前

He	has	worked	so
主詞	助動詞	動詞	句型

hard	**that** he definitely deserves the promotion.
副詞	that子句

Step 1 ➡ So+副詞hard移至句首。

Step 2 ➡ 主詞he移至助動詞has後。

倒裝句大變身！

Step 3 ➡ that子句不動，就會變成：

倒裝後

So	hard	has	he
句型	副詞	助動詞	主詞

worked	**that** he definitely deserves the promotion.
動詞	that子句

（他工作得這麼努力，當然值得獲得晉升。）

146

例3

倒裝前

It	~~(did)~~	rained	so
主詞	助動詞	動詞	句型

heavily	**that** they had to close the airport.
副詞	that子句

Step 1 ➡ **So**+副詞**hard**移至句首。

 倒裝句大變身！

Step 2 ➡ 主詞**it**往後移，並加入助動詞**did**。

Step 3 ➡ **that**子句不動，就會變成：

倒裝後

So	hard	did	it
句型	副詞	助動詞	主詞

rain	**that** they had to close the airport.
動詞	that子句

（雨下得那麼大，使得他們必須將機場關閉。）

前半句的主要動詞rain，
接在助動詞之後要去掉ed喔！

原來如此！

2 such ... that ... 倒裝：

例1

倒裝前

主詞	be動詞	句型	名詞片語	that子句
It	is	such	a beautiful day	that we should go picnicking in the park.

Step 1 → Such+名詞片語a beautiful day移至句首。

Step 2 → 主詞it往後移至be動詞is之後。

倒裝句大變身！

Step 3 → that子句不動，就會變成：

倒裝後

句型	名詞片語	助動詞	主詞	that子句
Such	a beautiful day	is	it	that we should go picnicking in the park.

（今天天氣如此美好，我們應該要去公園野餐。）

例2

倒裝前

主詞	助動詞	動詞	句型	名詞片語
You	had	made	such	a great effort to achieve the goal

that子句
that you should all be proud of yourselves.

倒裝句大變身！

Step 1 → Such+名詞片語a great effort to achieve the goal移至句首。

Step 2 → 主詞you往後移至助動詞had之後。

148

Step 3 ➡ that子句不動，就會變成：

倒裝後

Such	a great effort to achieve the goal	had	you	made
句型	名詞片語	助動詞	主詞	動詞

that you should all be proud of yourselves.
that子句

（你們為了達成目標做了這麼大的努力，你們全都應該以自己為傲。）

例3

倒裝前

He	(did)	made	such	a big mistake
主詞	助動詞	動詞	句型	名詞片語

that he deserves to be punished.
that子句

Step 1 ➡ Such+名詞片語a big mistake移至句首。

Step 2 ➡ 主詞he往後移，並加上助動詞did。 倒裝句大變身！

Step 3 ➡ that子句不動，就會變成：

倒裝前

Such	a big mistake	did	he	make
句型	名詞片語	助動詞	主詞	動詞

that he deserves to be punished.
that子句

（他犯了這麼大的錯，理應受罰。）

將下列句子以倒裝句改寫

1. He arrived so late that he missed the concert.

   _____

2. It is such a beautiful day that I don't want to waste it in the office.

   _____

3. My sister plays the piano so well that she can make a great pianist.

   _____

   _____

4. It is such a big decision that we must take everything into consideration.

   _____

5. He told me such a hilarious joke that I couldn't help burst out laughing.

   _____

   _____

ANSWER

1. So late did he arrive that he missed the concert.
2. Such a beautiful day it is that I don't want to waste it in the office.
3. So well does my sister play the piano that she can make a great pianist.
4. Such a big decision it is that we must take everything into consideration.
5. Such a hilarious joke did he tell me that I couldn't help burst out laughing.

地方副詞倒裝句構

地方副詞倒裝句構即所謂的「完全倒裝句構」。在句子中表示「地方」或「方向」的副詞如out, in, up, down, off, here, there等或副詞片語，可以移到句首做倒裝。

1 動詞為be動詞的倒裝：

例1

倒裝前

The students	are	there.
主詞	be動詞	地方副詞

倒裝後

There	are	the students.
地方副詞	be動詞	主詞

（學生們在那兒。）

例2

倒裝前

My passport	is	here.
主詞	be動詞	地方副詞

倒裝後

Here	is	my passport.
地方副詞	be動詞	主詞

（我的護照在這裡。）

2 動詞為不及物動詞的倒裝：

地方副詞（片語）移到句首，主詞與動詞倒裝。

例1

倒裝前

The bus	comes	here.
主詞	不及物動詞	地方副詞

倒裝後

Here	comes	the bus.
地方副詞	不及物動詞	主詞

（公車來了。）

例2

倒裝前

The boy	fell	fell off the tree.
主詞	不及物動詞	地方副詞

倒裝後

Off the tree	fell	the boy.
地方副詞	不及物動詞	主詞

（男孩從樹上摔下來。）

例3

倒裝前

The rain	poured	down	for the whole week.
主詞	不及物動詞	地方副詞	時間

倒裝後

Down	poured	the rain	for the whole week.
地方副詞	不及物動詞	主詞	時間

（雨傾盆下了一整個星期。）

重點筆記

Tips

★句子中的主詞若為代名詞，做倒裝句時，副詞移到句首，但主詞（代名詞）與動詞不倒裝。

例1

倒裝前

She	is	here.
主詞	be動詞	副詞

倒裝後

Here	she	is.
副詞	主詞	be動詞

（公車來了。）

例2

倒裝前

He	sat	there.
主詞	動詞	副詞

倒裝後

There	he	sat.
副詞	主詞	動詞

（他就坐在那裡。）

例3

倒裝前

It	hid	behind the bush.
主詞	動詞	副詞

倒裝後

Behind the bush	it	hid
副詞	主詞	動詞

（牠就躲在樹叢後。）

例4

倒裝前

He	walked	along the river.
主詞	動詞	副詞

倒裝後

Along the river	he	walked.
副詞	主詞	動詞

（他沿著河散步。）

153

3 be動詞＋分詞的倒裝：

地方副詞移到句首，「be動詞＋分詞」與主詞倒裝。

【 進行式：be動詞＋現在分詞 】

倒裝時，字序為：**副詞＋be動詞＋Ving＋名詞**

▼

例1

倒裝前

A man	is hiding	behind the door.
主詞	動詞（be+Ving）	地方副詞

倒裝後

Behind the door	is hiding	a man.
地方副詞	動詞（be+Ving）	主詞

（躲在門後的是一個男人。）

例2

倒裝前

Your mom and dad	were waiting	at the lobby.
主詞	動詞(be+Ving)	地方副詞

倒裝後

At the lobby	were waiting	your mom and dad.
地方副詞	動詞(be+Ving)	主詞

（在大廳等著的是你的爸爸媽媽。）

【 進行式：be動詞＋過去分詞 】

倒裝時，字序為：**副詞＋be動詞＋Vp.p.＋名詞**

▶

例1

倒裝前

His works of art	were displayed	in the gallery.
主詞	動詞(be+Vp.p.)	地方副詞

倒裝後

In the gallery	were displayed	his works of art.
地方副詞	動詞(be+Vp.p.)	主詞

（在美術館裡展覽的是他的藝術作品。）

例2

倒裝前

The Maldives	are situated	in the Indian Ocean, south-southwest of India.
主詞	動詞(be+Vp.p.)	地方副詞

倒裝後

In the Indian Ocean, south-southwest of India	are situated	the Maldives.
地方副詞	動詞(be+Vp.p.)	主詞

（在印度西南南方的印度洋上，是馬爾地夫群島所在之處。）

將下列句子以倒裝句改寫

1. Mary comes here.

_____

2. There was a princess named Snow White once.

_____

3. Our hotel is not far away from the Old Town Square.

_____

4. The body of the victim was hid in the trunk of the car.

_____

5. The birthday girl came down in a white princess dress.

_____

ANSWER

1. Here comes Mary.
2. Once there was a princess named Snow White.
3. Not far away from the Old Town Square is our hotel.
4. In the trunk of the car was hid the body of the victim.
5. Down came the birthday girl in a white princess dress.

假設倒裝句構

　　假設倒裝句是用在需要特別強調假設語氣的情況，將具有「假設含義」的助動詞移到句首，取代表示假設的if，以達到強調目的。

1 與現在事實相反的假設倒裝句：

倒裝時，去掉連接詞If，把were移至句首。

【基本句型】

Were＋主詞＋……, 主詞＋ $\left\{\begin{array}{l}\text{would}\\\text{could}\\\text{should}\\\text{might}\end{array}\right\}$ ＋現在完成式

例1

在倒裝句裡，我就會被省略！

倒裝前

If	they	were	here,	they would also be proud of you.
連接詞	主詞	Be動詞	地方副詞	主要子句

倒裝後

~~If~~	Were	they	here,	they would also be proud of you.
連接詞	Be動詞	主詞	地方副詞	主要子句

（如果他們在這裡的話，也會為你感到驕傲。）

例2

在倒裝句裡，我就會被省略！

倒裝前

If	it	were	not for your help,	we couldn't make it.
連接詞	主詞	Be動詞	副詞	主要子句

倒裝後

~~If~~	Were	it	not for your help,	we couldn't make it.
連接詞	Be動詞	主詞	副詞	主要子句

（要不是有你的幫忙，我們不會成功的。）

★使用一般動詞與現在事實相反的假設句(i.e. If I had a car, I'd be happy.)，
　較少使用倒裝句來做強調。

2 與過去事實相反的假設倒裝句：

倒裝時，去掉連接詞If，把助動詞had移至句首。

【基本句型】

Had＋主詞＋......, 主詞＋ $\begin{cases} \text{would} \\ \text{could} \\ \text{should} \\ \text{might} \end{cases}$ ＋現在完成式

例1
倒裝前

If	the flight	had	not	been delayed,
連接詞	主詞	助動詞	否定詞	主要動詞

we would have already arrived.
主要子句

倒裝後

~~If~~	Had	the flight	not	been delayed,
~~連接詞~~	助動詞	主詞	否定詞	主要動詞

we would have already arrived.
主要子句

（如果班機沒有被延遲的話，我們早就已經到了。）

例2

在倒裝句裡，我就會被省略！

倒裝前

If	you	had	helped him,	he could have succeeded.
連接詞	主詞	助動詞	主要動詞	主要子句

倒裝後

If	Had	you	helped him,	he could have succeeded.
連接詞	助動詞	主詞	主要動詞	主要子句

（如果你有幫他的話，他可能已經成功了。）

3 表示未來「萬一」的假設倒裝句：

【were to的假設句】

倒裝時，去掉連接詞If，把be動詞Were移至句首。

句型：Were＋主詞＋不定詞，主詞＋$\begin{Bmatrix} \text{would} \\ \text{could} \\ \text{should} \\ \text{might} \end{Bmatrix}$＋原形動詞

例1

在倒裝句裡，我就會被省略！

倒裝前

If	he	were	to visit me,	he would call me in advance.
連接詞	主詞	be動詞	主要動詞	主要子句

倒裝後

If	Were	he	to visit me,	he would call me in advance.
連接詞	be動詞	主詞	主要動詞	主要子句

（如果他要來看我，他會先打電話給我。）

例2

在倒裝句裡，我就會被省略！

倒裝前

If	the world	were	to end tomorrow,	what would you do today?
連接詞	主詞	be動詞	主要動詞	主要子句

倒裝後

~~if~~	Were	the world	to end tomorrow,	what would you do today?
~~連接詞~~	be動詞	主詞	主要動詞	主要子句

（如果世界明天就是末日，你今天會做什麼？）

【should的假設句】

倒裝時，去掉連接詞If，把助動詞Should移至句首。

句型：Should＋主詞＋……，主詞＋$\begin{cases} \text{would} \\ \text{could} \\ \text{should} \\ \text{might} \end{cases}$＋原形動詞

例1

在倒裝句裡，我就會被省略！

倒裝前

If	it	should	rain tomorrow,	the football game would be put off.
連接詞	主詞	助動詞	主要動詞	主要子句

倒裝後

~~If~~	Should	it	rain tomorrow,	the football game would be put off.
~~連接詞~~	助動詞	主詞	主要動詞	主要子句

（萬一明天下雨的話，足球賽就會被延後。）

例1

在倒裝句裡，我就會被省略！

倒裝前

If	he	should	come again,	you should call the police.
連接詞	主詞	助動詞	主要動詞	主要子句

倒裝後

~~If~~	Should	he	come again,	you should call the police.
連接詞	助動詞	主詞	主要動詞	主要子句

（萬一他要是再來的話，你們應該就要報警。）

文法練習站 ❺

將下列句子以倒裝句改寫

1. If you were in my shoes, you wouldn't say that.

   _____

2. If the sun were to explode, the earth would be destroyed.

   _____

3. If she hadn't had plastic surgery, she wouldn't have looked so attractive.

   _____

4. If we had set off earlier, we wouldn't have been trapped in traffic.

   _____

5. If he should cheat in the exam, he could be expelled from school.

   _____

ANSWER

1. Were you in my shoes, you wouldn't say that.
2. Were the sun to explode, the earth would be destroyed.
3. Had she not had plastic surgery, she wouldn't have looked so attractive.
4. Had we set off earlier, we wouldn't have been trapped in traffic.
5. Should he cheat in the exam, he could be expelled from school.

文法總複習

A 選擇

1. (　) Next to the shopping mall _____ build a hotel.
   A. they can　B. will they　C. they should　D. had we

2. (　) On the other side of the street _____.
   A. stand an old lady
   B. a boy is waiting
   C. some people are taking pictures
   D. waited the boy's mother

3. (　) _____ impatient to his patients.
   A. Been had the doctor never
   B. Had the doctor never been
   C. Never had the doctor been
   D. Had been the doctor never

4. (　) _____ in this world can I feel so secure as in home.
   A. Nowhere　B. Nothing　C. Sometimes　D. Never

5. (　) Not for a moment _____ the authenticity of his academic credentials.
   A. we are doubting　　　B. we have ever doubted
   C. did we doubt　　　　D. we doubted

6. (　) _____ selfless is he that he deserves all my respect.
   A. Such　　B. So　　C. How　　D. Even

7. (　) _____ a great exhibition it is that you shouldn't miss it.
   A. So　　B. What　　C. How　　D. Such

8. (　) Never before in similar situation _____.
   A. had a Minister leave the municipal meeting midway
   B. a Minister has left the municipal midway
   C. did a Minister have left the municipal midway
   D. a Minister had left the municipal midway

B 以倒裝句翻譯下列句子

1. 唯有當你去過倫敦塔橋，你才能説你去過倫敦。(Tower Bridge)

_____

2. 我哪裡都找不到我的護照。

_____

3. 他從來不滿意我所做的任何事。(pleased)

_____

4. 我很少看到我爸爸哭。

_____

5. 無論在任何情況下我都不會背叛我的國家。

_____

6. Mary不但是個美食家，她還是個大胃王。(foodie/big eater)

_____

7. 我兒子絕對不敢像那樣跟我頂嘴。(dare/talk back)

_____

ANSWER

A. 選擇

1. B 2. D 3. C 4. A 5. C 6. B 7. D 8. A

B. 翻譯下列句子

1. Only when you visit the Tower Bridge can you say you have been to London.
2. Nowhere can I find my passport.
3. Never is he pleased with anything I do.
4. Seldom do I see my father cry.
5. Under no circumstances will I betray my country.
6. Not only is Mary a foodie, but she is also a big eater.
7. Never would my son dare to talk to me like that.

Lesson 7

強調語氣Ⅲ──
比較級與讓步子句

「我那麼喜歡她，她卻不看我一眼！」
Much as I like her,
she keeps ignoring me.

強調語氣III——
比較級與讓步子句

除了分裂句構及倒裝句構之外，我們還可以用比較級與讓步子句來表示強調語氣。這兩種句型是以「詞組移位」的方式來強調句子中的某些元素，也就是將需要強調的部分移至句首，以達到強調目的。

 比較級的強調

當句子中有比較級時，可以將想要強調的詞組移到句首，並在前面加上定冠詞the，以表示「越……越……」。

句型：The ＋比較級＋……，the ＋比較級＋……

1 受詞移位

改造句子以強調受詞時，將有比較級的受詞詞組移到句首，前面加上the，其餘詞序不變。

例1 改造前

Youbuy	more items	and	you'll get	more discount.
主詞+動詞	受詞 （含比較級詞組）	連接詞	主詞+動詞	受詞 （含比較級詞組）

Step 1 ─── 找出含有比較級的詞組，前面加 **the**。
　　　　　 the more items、**the more discount**

Step 2 ─── 把改造過的詞組移到子句的最前面。

Step 3 ─── 把中間的連接詞改成逗號，就會變成：

強調語氣，
句子大變身

改造後

The more items	you buy,	the more discount	you'll get.
受詞 （含比較級詞組）	主詞＋動詞 （加逗號）	受詞（含比較級詞組）	主詞＋動詞

（買越多件，優惠越多。）

例2

改造前

I eat	more food,	and	I lose	more weight.
主詞＋動詞	受詞 （含比較級詞組）	連接詞	主詞＋動詞	受詞 （含比較級詞組）

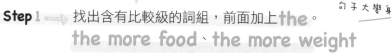

強調語氣，
句子大變身

Step 1 ─── 找出含有比較級的詞組，前面加上 **the**。
　　　　　 the more food、**the more weight**

Step 2 ─── 把改造過的詞組移到子句的最前面。

Step 3 ─── 把中間的連接詞 **and** 改成逗號，就會變成：

改造後

The more food	I eat,	the more weight	I lose.
受詞 （含比較級詞組）	主詞＋動詞 （加逗號）	受詞 （含比較級詞組）	主詞＋動詞

（我吃得越多，體重掉得越多。）

將下列句子以比較級強調句改寫

1. We use more plastic products, and we create more pollution.

    _____

    _____

2. If we have more children, we will need a bigger house.

    _____

    _____

3. When you eat more junk food, your body takes in more unnecessary calories.

    _____

    _____

4. When you tell more lies, people will have less respect for you.

    _____

    _____

5. He makes more money, and he donates more money to the charities.

    _____

    _____

ANSWER

1. The more plastic products we use, the more pollution we create.
2. The more children we have, the bigger house we'll need.
3. The more junk food you eat, the more unnecessary calories your body takes in.
4. The more lies you tell, the less respect people will have for you.
5. The more money he makes, the more money he donates to the charities.

2 形容詞移位

強調形容詞時，將比較級形容詞組移到句首，前面加上the，其餘詞序不變。

例1

改造前

When	you are	fatter,	you become	less healthy.
連接詞	主詞＋be動詞	形容詞比較級	主詞＋動詞	形容詞比較級

Step 1 ➡ 找出含有比較級的詞組，前面加上 **the**。
the fatter、**the less healthy**

強調語氣，
句子大變身

Step 2 ➡ 把改造過的詞組移到子句的最前面。

Step 3 ➡ 把連接詞When去掉，就會變成：

改造後

The fatter	you are,	the less healthy	you become.
形容詞比較級	主詞＋be動詞（加逗號）	形容詞比較級	主詞＋動詞

（你越胖，就變得越不健康。）

例2

改造前

When	we are	older,	we should be	wiser.
連接詞	主詞＋be動詞	形容詞比較級	主詞＋動詞	形容詞比較級

Step 1 ➡ 找出含有比較級的詞組，前面加上 **the**。
the older、**the wiser**

強調語氣，
句子大變身

Step 2 → 把改造過的詞組移到子句的最前面。

Step 3 → 把中間的連接詞 and 去掉逗號，就會變成：

改造後

The older	we are,	the wiser	we should be.
形容詞比較級	主詞＋be動詞（加逗號）	形容詞比較級	主詞+動詞

（我們年紀越大，就應該越有智慧。）

 文法練習站 ❷

將下列句子以比較級強調句改寫

1. My grandfather gets older, and he becomes more energetic.

   _____

2. When the kids get wilder, I become more impatient.

   _____

3. If you eat healthier, your body will be stronger.

   _____

4. When the temperature is higher, you will feel hotter.

   _____

5. The thunder was louder and the children were more frightened.

   _____

ANSWER

1. The older my grandfather gets, the more energetic he becomes.
2. The wilder the kids get, the more impatient I become.
3. The healthier you eat, the stronger your body will be.
4. The higher the temperature is, the hotter you will feel.
5. The louder the thunder was, the more frightened the children were.

3 副詞移位

強調副詞時，將有比較級的副詞詞組移到句首，前面加上the，其餘詞序不變。

例1 改造前

If	he uses his time	better,	he will work	more efficiently.
連接詞	主詞＋動詞	副詞比較級	主詞＋動詞	副詞比較級

Step 1 → 找出含有副詞比較級的詞組，前面加上 **the**。
the better、the more efficiently

Step 2 → 把改造過的詞組移到子句的最前面。

強調語氣，句子大變身

Step 3 → 把連接詞 **If** 去掉，就會變成：

改造後

The better	he uses his time,	the more efficiently	he will work.
副詞比較級	主詞＋動詞（加逗號）	副詞比較級	主詞＋動詞

（你時間管理得越好，工作越有效率。）

例2 改造前

If	you work	more efficiently,	you can get your job done	faster.
連接詞	主詞＋動詞	副詞比較級	主詞＋動詞	副詞比較級

Step 1 → 找出含有副詞比較級的詞組，前面加上 **the**。
the more efficiently、the faster

強調語氣，句子大變身

Step 2 把改造過的詞組移到子句的最前面。

Step 3 把連接詞**If**去掉，就會變成：

改造後

The more efficiently	you work,	the faster	you can get your job done.
副詞比較級	主詞＋動詞（加逗號）	副詞比較級	主詞＋動詞

（你工作得越有效率，你就能更快完成工作。）

★ 同一個句子裡可以有兩種不同詞組移位的比較級強調子句。

例1 改造前

You drink	more alcohol,	and you'll die	sooner.
主詞＋動詞	受詞詞組（含形容詞比較級）	連接詞＋主詞＋動詞	副詞比較級

強調語氣，句子大變身

Step 1 找出含有比較級的詞組，前面加上**the**。
the more alcohol、the faster

Step 2 把改造過的詞組移到子句的最前面。

Step 3 把連接詞and去掉，就會變成：

改造後

The more alcohol	you drink,	the sooner	you'll die.
受詞詞組（含形容詞比較級）	主詞＋動詞（加逗號）	副詞比較級	主詞＋動詞

（你酒喝得愈多死得愈快。）

例2

改造前

If	you are	more prepared,	you will have	more confidence.
連接詞	主詞＋be動詞	主詞補語（含形容詞比較級）	主詞＋動詞	受詞詞組（含形容詞比較級）

Step 1 ➡ 找出含有副詞比較級的詞組，前面加上 the。

the more prepared、the more confidence

Step 2 ➡ 把改造過的詞組移到子句的最前面。

Step 3 ➡ 把連接詞 If 去掉，就會變成：

改造後

The more prepared	you are,	the more confidence	you'll have.
主詞補語（含形容詞比較級）	主詞＋動詞（加逗號）	受詞詞組（含形容詞比較級）	主詞＋動詞

（你越是準備充分，你就會有越多的信心。）

文法練習站 ❸

將下列句子以比較級強調句改寫

1. If you did the homework more carefully, you would make fewer mistakes.

_____

_____

2. We learn more, and we know less.

_____

_____

3. If you write faster, your handwriting is more careless.

_____

_____

4. We talk more, and we understand each other better.

_____

_____

5. If you describe your lost suitcase more specifically, we may find it soon.

_____

_____

ANSWER

1. The more carefully you did the homework, the fewer mistakes you would make.
2. The more we learn, the less we know.
3. The faster you write, the more careless your handwriting is.
4. The more we talk, the better we understand each other.
5. The more specifically you describe your lost suitcase, the sooner we may find it.

 讓步子句的強調

　　表示矛盾的although引導一個具「矛盾含義」的子句，要強調讓步子句中的特定元素時，以as取代although或though，並將句子中需要強調的元素移位至句首，以達到強調目的。

1 名詞移位：

當although或though引導be動詞的子句，而be動詞後的補語為名詞時，將名詞詞組移到句首，並以as取代although，其餘詞序不變。

例1

改造前

Although	he is	a millionaire,	he is quite thrifty.
連接詞	主詞＋be動詞	主詞補語（名詞）	主要子句

Step 1 把名詞 a millionaire 移到句首。

Step 2 把 Although 去掉、換成 as。

強調語氣，句子大變身

Step 3 主要子句不動，就會變成：

改造後

A millionaire	as	he is,	he is quite thrifty.
主詞補語（名詞）	（取代Although）	主詞＋be動詞（加逗號）	主要子句

（儘管他是個百萬富翁，他卻相當節儉。）

例2

改造前

Though	she is	a fulltime mother,	she never gives up her dreams for her children.
連接詞	主詞＋be動詞	主詞補語（名詞）	主要子句

強調語氣，句子大變身

Step 1 把名詞 a fulltime mother 移到句首。

Step 2 把 though 去掉、換成 as。

Step 3 主要子句不動，就會變成：

改造後

A fulltime mother	as	she is	she never gives up her dreams for her children.
主詞補語 （名詞）	（取代though）	主詞＋be動詞 （加逗號）	主要子句

（雖然她是個全職母親，卻從未為孩子放棄過自己的夢想。）

文法練習站 ❹

以強調語氣改寫下列句子

1. Although he is a boss, he works even harder than his employees.

   _____

   _____

2. Although the man is a beggar, he never takes anything that doesn't belong to him.

   _____

   _____

3. Although it is a great job offer, I can't accept it.

   _____

   _____

4. Although I am your mother, you shouldn't take everything I do for you for granted.

   _____

   _____

5. Although she is a three-year-old child, she plays tennis like a professional.

   _____

   _____

ANSWER

1. A boss as he is, he works even harder than his employees.
2. A beggar as the man is, he never takes anything that doesn't belong to him.
3. A great job offer as it is, I can't accept it.
4. Your mother as I am, you shouldn't take everything I do for you for granted.
5. A three-year-old child as she is, she plays tennis like a professional.

形容詞移句首，再用as取代 though/although，簡單啦！

原來如此！

2 形容詞移位：

　　當although或though引導be動詞子句，且be動詞後的補語為形容詞時，將形容詞詞組移到句首，並以as取代although，其餘詞序不變。

例1

改造前

Although	it is	nice,	I don't want to go out.
連接詞	主詞＋be動詞	主詞補語（形容詞）	主要子句

Step 1 ⟶ 把形容詞**nice**移到句首。

Step 2 ⟶ 把**Although**去掉、換成**as**。

強調語氣，句子大變身

Step 3 ⟶ 主要子句不動，就會變成：

改造後

Nice	as	it is,	I don't want to go out.
主詞補語（形容詞）	（取代Although）	主詞＋be動詞（加逗號）	主要子句

（雖然天氣很好，但我並不想出門。）

177

例2

改造前

Although	he is	seriously ill,	he is still eager to live.
連接詞	主詞＋be動詞	主詞補語（形容詞）	主要子句

Step 1 → 把形容詞的詞組 seriously ill 移到句首。

Step 2 → 把 Although 去掉、換成 as。

強調語氣，
句子大變身

Step 3 → 主要子句不動，就會變成：

改造後

Seriously ill	as	he is,	he is still eager to live.
主詞補語（形容詞）	（取代Although）	主詞＋be動詞（加逗號）	主要子句

（儘管他病得很重，他仍渴望活下去。）

文法練習站 ❺

以強調語氣改寫下列句子

1. Although he was tired, he was not allowed to take a break.

   _____

   _____

2. Although she is ill, she insists on going to work.

   _____

   _____

3. Though the problem was tough, he solved it effortlessly.

_____

_____

4. Though my sister was reluctant, she let me share the room with her.

_____

_____

5. Although the atmosphere was tense, she nerved herself to ask the question.

_____

_____

ANSWER

1. Tired as he was, he was not allowed to take a break.
2. Ill as she is, she insists on going to work.
3. Tough as the problem was, he solved it effortlessly.
4. Reluctant as my sister was, she let me share the room with her.
5. Tense as the atmosphere was, she nerved herself to ask the question.

3▶ 副詞移位：

　　although的句子中，有修飾動詞的副詞時，將副詞移到句首，並以as取代although，其餘詞序不變。

原來如此！

副詞移句首，再as取代though/although，超好子記！

例1

改造前

Although	he tried	hard,	he failed to reach his goal.
連接詞	主詞＋動詞	副詞	主要子句

Step 1 ➡ 把副詞 **hard** 移到句首。

Step 2 ➡ 把 **Although** 去掉、換成 **as**。

Step 3 ➡ 主要子句不動，就會變成：

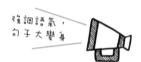

改造後

Hard	as	he tried,	he failed to reach his goals.
副詞	（取代Although）	主詞＋動詞（加逗號）	主要子句

（儘管他努力嘗試，仍然無法達成目標。）

例2

改造前

Although	she speaks English	fluently,	she can't read it.
連接詞	主詞＋動詞	副詞	主要子句

Step 1 ➡ 把副詞 **fluently** 移到句首。

Step 2 ➡ 把 **Although** 去掉、換成 **as**。

Step 3 ➡ 主要子句不動，就會變成：

改造後

Fluently	as	she speaks English,	she can't read it.
副詞	（取代Although）	主詞＋動詞 （加逗號）	主要子句

（儘管她英文説得很流利，她卻不會看字。）

重點筆記

★ although 子句中的動詞沒有特別的副詞做修飾，卻需要表示強調時，加入副詞much（表示「很」），將much移到句首，再將as取代although，其餘詞序不變。

例1

改造前

Although	I love you	(much),	I can't do everything for you.
連接詞	主詞＋動詞	副詞	主要子句

原來如此！

much可以當作表示程度的副詞。

Step 1 ⟹ 補一個副詞 **much**、把它移到句首。

Step 2 ⟹ 把**Although**去掉、換成**as**。

Step 3 ⟹ 主要子句不動，就會變成：

強調語氣，句子大變身

改造後

Much	as	I love you,	I can't do everything for you.
副詞	（取代Although）	主詞＋動詞 （加逗號）	主要子句

（儘管我很愛你，我也不能幫你做每件事。）

例2

改造前

Though	he needed a new computer	(much),	he couldn't afford it.
連接詞	主詞＋動詞	副詞	主要子句

Step 1 → 補一個副詞**much**、把它移到句首。

Step 2 → 把**Though**去掉、換成**as**。

強調語氣，
句子大變身

Step 3 → 主要子句不動，就會變成：

改造後

Much	as	he needed a new computer,	he couldn't afford it.
副詞	（取代Though）	主詞＋動詞（加逗號）	主要子句

（雖然他很需要一台新電腦，他卻買不起。）

文法練習站 ❻

以強調句改寫下列句子

1. Though I apologized sincerely, she wouldn't forgive me.

   _____

   _____

2. Though we regret the inconvenience, we can't do anything about it.

   _____

   _____

3. Although she ran fast, she missed the train.

   _____

   _____

4. Although I have tried, I failed my parents' expectation.

_____

_____

5. Though he works diligently, his boss still finds fault with him all the time.

_____

_____

ANSWER

1. Sincerely as I apologized, she wouldn't forgive me.
2. Much as we regret the inconvenience, we can't do anything about it.
3. Fast as she ran, she missed the train.
4. Much as I have tried, I failed my parents' expectation.
5. Diligently as he works, his boss still finds fault with him all the time.

4 動詞移位：

　　動詞移位的情形只會出現在當although的句子有助動詞may（可以）時。將may後面的動詞移到句首，並以as取代although，其餘詞序不變。

例1

改造前

Although	you	may	stay,	keep your hands off anything in this room.
連接詞	主詞	助動詞	動詞	主要子句

原來如此！

句子有may這個助動詞時，才可以將動詞往前移來改造！

183

Step 1 ➡ 找到動詞**stay**、把它移到句首。

Step 2 ➡ 把**Although**去掉、換成**as**。

Step 3 ➡ 主要子句不動，就會變成：

強調語氣，
句子大變身

改造後

Stay	as	you may,	keep your hands off anything in this room.
動詞		主詞＋助動詞（加逗號）	主要子句

（儘管你可以留下來，這個房間內的任何東西你都不能碰。）

例2

改造前

Though	she	may	leave,	she can't take the boy with her.
連接詞	主詞	助動詞	動詞	主要子句

Step 1 ➡ 找到動詞**leave**、把它移到句首。

Step 2 ➡ 把**Although**去掉、換成**as**。

Step 3 ➡ 主要子句不動，就會變成：

強調語氣，
句子大變身

改造後

Leave	as	she may,	she can't take the boy with her.
動詞		主詞＋助動詞（加逗號）	主要子句

（她雖然可以離開，但她不能帶走這個男孩兒。）

文法練習站 ❼

以強調句改寫下列句子

1. Although you may use my car, you have to return it by tomorrow.

   _____

   _____

2. Though they may wait in the room, they have to stay quiet.

   _____

   _____

3. Although he may go with us, he has to pay for himself.

   _____

   _____

4. Though she may use the gym, she must abide by the dress code.

   _____

   _____

5. Although you may have a party here, you have to clean after yourselves.

   _____

   _____

ANSWER

1. Use my car as you may, you have to return it by tomorrow.
2. Wait in the room as they may, they have to stay quiet.
3. Go with us as he may, he has to pay for himself.
4. Use the gym as she may, she must abide by the dress code.
5. Have a party here as you may, you have to clean after yourselves.

文法總複習

A 選擇

1. (　) Expensive _____ it is, I'm going to buy it.
   A. although　　B. as　　C. even　　D. though

2. (　) _____ as she realized her mistake, she refused to apologize.
   A. More　　B. Lot　　C. Even　　D. Much

3. (　) Try as you _____, you can't change the results.
   A. may　　B. like　　C. wish　　D. did

4. (　) _____ as I am, this chocolate is also too sweet for me.
   A. Sweet　　B. I like cake　　C. A sweet tooth　　D. Quickly

5. (　) Late as it _____, there are still a lot of people in the night market.
   A. may　　B. is　　C. will be　　D. comes

6. (　) The more _____ he feels, the more coffee he drinks.
   A. sleepy　　B. asleep　　C. sleeping　　D. sleeps

7. (　) _____ as Lily is, she is unkind.
   A. Study　　B. Carefully　　C. May　　D. Beautiful

8. (　) A scientist as John Louis _____, he wrote beautiful poems.
   A. may　　B. was　　C. does　　D. looked

B 以強調句翻譯下列句子

1. 雖然他病了，但是他不去看醫生。

_____

2. 儘管這個教授很嚴格，他卻深受學生們喜愛。(strict/popular)

_____

3. 雖然我很想出國旅遊，但我忙得沒辦法這麼做。

_____

4. 你不守承諾越多次，你的孩子就越不相信你。(keep one's word)

_____

5. 你擁有的權力越大，你所要承擔的責任也就越大。
   (possess / responsibility)

_____

6. 越往高處走，就會越冷。

_____

7. 雖然你可以在家開派對，但是派對後要整理乾淨。

_____

ANSWER

A. 選擇

1. B   2. D   3. A   4. C   5. B   6. A   7. D   8. B

B. 以強調句翻譯下列句子

1. Ill as he was, he wouldn't go to the doctor.
2. Strict as this professor is, he is very popular with the students.
3. Much as I want to take a trip abroad, I am too busy to do so.
4. The more times you fail to keep your word, the less your children will believe you.
5. The more power you possess, the more responsibility you are to take.
6. The higher you go, the cooler it is.
7. Have parties at home as you may, you have to clean up after the parties.

Lesson 8

分詞構句

「看著她，我感覺心跳加快。」
Looking at her, I feel my heart is racing.

分詞構句

所謂的分詞構句，就是利用分詞─即現在分詞及過去分詞，簡化從屬子句，使之成為分詞片語：將形容詞子句簡化「分詞形容詞片語」、副詞子句簡化「副詞片語」，達到修飾或說明主要子句的目的。

為什麼要簡化從屬子句呢？當我們為了將語意表達得更完整，而以連接詞把兩個獨立的句子連接起來後，往往會讓句子顯得十分冗長。因此出現了分詞構句，用少少幾個字就能達到一樣的描述效果。

分詞構句的關鍵，在於主動與被動的分辨。分清楚主被動，再以既定語法規則將副詞子句化繁為簡，就能靈活運用分詞構句了。

什麼時候可以用分詞構句

分詞構句的目的，是要將兩個主詞相同的句子簡化合併。因此當連接詞連接的前後兩個句子主詞相同時，就可以用分詞構句來簡化。

要將哪一個句子簡化？

會簡化成分詞片語的句子，通常是用來修飾、描述或補充說明，以使另一個句子語意更加完整的副詞子句。

例1 改造前

When	I	looked at the food,	I	started to feel hungry.
連接詞	主詞	動詞	主詞	動詞

Step 1 ➡ 確認前後兩個子句相同（都是 **I** ）、去掉前半子句的主詞。

Step 2 ➡ 去掉連接詞 **when**。

Step 3 ➡ 把前半子句的動詞變成 **V-ing** 形式，就會變成：

改造後

~~When~~	~~I~~	**Looking** at the food,	I	started to feel hungry.
連接詞	主詞	動詞	主詞	動詞

（看著眼前的菜餚，我便開始感到餓了。）

例2 改造前

Because	he	didn't	know what to do,	he	asked a stranger for help.
連接詞	主詞	否定詞	動詞	主詞	動詞

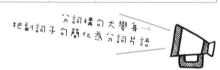

Step 1 ➡ 確認前後兩個子句相同（都是 **he** ）、去掉前半子句的主詞。

Step 2 ➡ 去掉連接詞 **Because**。

Step 3 ➡ 把否定詞 **didn't** 改為 **Not**。

Step 4 ➡ 把前半子句的動詞變成 **V-ing** 形式 **(knowing)**，就會變成：

191

改造後

When	+	Not	knowing what to do,	he	asked a stranger for help.
~~連接詞~~	主詞	否定詞	動詞	主詞	動詞

（因為不知道該怎麼辦，他於是向一個陌生人求助。）

例3 改造前

The man	died in a car crash,	and	he	left nothing to his wife and children.
主詞	動詞	連接詞	主詞	動詞

Step 1 ⟹ 確認前後兩個子句為同一人（都是**the man**）、去掉後半子句的主詞。

把副詞子句簡化為分詞片語
分詞構句大變身→

Step 2 ⟹ 去掉連接詞**and**。

Step 3 ⟹ 把前半子句的動詞變成**V-ing**形式**(leaving)**，就會變成：

改造後

The man	died in a car crash,	~~and~~	~~he~~	**leaving** nothing to his wife and children.
主詞	動詞	連接詞	~~主詞~~	動詞

（男子在一場車禍中離世，什麼也沒有留給妻子。）

形成分詞構句的方式

確認連接詞前後句子的兩個主詞相同時，就可以開始進行簡化。

Step 1 → 去掉副詞子句的主詞。

Step 2 → 省略連接詞。若要表示強調意味時,則保留連接詞。

Step 3 → 判斷副詞子句為主動語態或被動語態。

Step 4 → 若為否定句,則去掉助動詞,保留 **not** 或 **never**,置於分詞之前。

主動語態時,不分時態,將動詞改為現在分詞 V-ing。

原來如此!

Tips

重點筆記

❶ 副詞子句為be動詞,且有受詞時(即形容詞+介系詞+受詞),being可以跟主詞一起省略,若沒有受詞,則通常不省略

❷ 若為完成式,將助動詞改為having,保留過去分詞 V-p.p.

❸ 被動語態的分詞構句中,being常被省略,只留過去分詞

❹ 若為被動完成式,助動詞have改為having,保留been及過去分詞 V-p.p.

被動語態時,可以將be動詞改為being並省略,保留過去分詞 V-p.p.

原來如此!

1▸ 主動句

例1 改造前

Because	Jack	left his wallet behind,	he	was unable to pay for this meal.
連接詞	主詞	動詞	主詞	動詞

Step 1 ➡ 確認前後兩個子句為同一人（都是**Jack**）、
去掉前半子句的主詞。

把副詞子句簡化為分詞片語
分詞構句大變身→

Step 2 ➡ 去掉連接詞**Because**。

Step 3 ➡ 本句為主動語態→動詞變成**V-ing**形式**(leaving)**就會變成：

改造後

~~Because~~	~~Jack~~	**Leaving** his wallet behind,	Jack	was unable to pay for his meal.
連接詞	主詞	動詞	主詞	動詞

（因為忘記帶錢包，Jack無法付餐費。）

例2 改造前

Because	he	is tired of eating out,	he	decided to cook for himself.
連接詞	主詞	動詞	主詞	動詞

Step 1 ➡ 確認前後兩個子句為同一人（都是**he**）、
去掉前半子句的主詞。

Step 2 ➡ 去掉連接詞**Because**。

Step 3 ➡ 本句為主動語態→動詞變成 V-ing形式(being)。

Step 4 ➡ 動詞改成 Ving，可以省略，就會變成：

改造後

Because	he	(Being) tired of eating out,	he	decided to cook for himself.
連接詞	主詞	動詞	主詞	動詞

（因為厭倦外食，他決定給自己做飯。）

文法練習站 **1**

將下列句子以分詞構句改寫

1. As soon as the little boy saw his mother, he started to cry.

   _____

   _____

2. When I heard the song, I couldn't help singing along.

   _____

   _____

3. Because she is interested in English, she reads a lot of English novels.

   _____

   _____

4. After he knew there was a rat in the house, he preferred to stay outside.

   _____

   _____

5. Because I am your father, I am responsible for your behavior.

_____

_____

ANSWER

1. Seeing his mother, the little boy started to cry.
2. Hearing the song, I couldn't help singing along.
3. (Being) interested in English, she reads a lot of English novels.
4. Knowing there was a rat in the house, he preferred to stay outside.
5. Being your father, I am responsible for your behavior.

2 被動句

例1 改造前

Because	Catherine	was transferred to the headquarters,
連接詞	主詞	動詞

she	now has to spend one more hour commuting to work.
主詞	動詞

↓

Step 1 ⟶ 確認前後兩個子句為同一人（都是**Catherine**）、去掉前半子句的主詞。

Step 2 ⟶ 去掉連接詞**Because**。

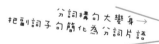
把副詞子句簡化為分詞片語 分詞構句大變身→

Step 3 ⟶ 本句為被動語態→動詞變成**Being**＋**V-p.p.(being transferred)** 形式：

Step 4 ⟶ **be**動詞改成**Ving**，可以省略，就會變成：

改造後

~~Because~~	~~Catherine~~	(Being) Transferred to the headquarters,
連接詞	主詞	動詞

Catherine	now has to spend one more hour commuting to work.
主詞	動詞

（因為被調到總公司，Catherine現在得多花一小時通勤上班。）

例2 改造前

Because	I	am accompanied by the bodyguards,
連接詞	主詞	動詞

I	felt very secure.
主詞	動詞

把副詞子句簡化為分詞片語
分詞構句大變身→

Step 1 ➡ 確認前後兩個子句為同一人（都是**I**）、去掉前半子句的主詞。

Step 2 ➡ 去掉連接詞**Because**，

Step 3 ➡ 本句為被動語態→動詞變成**Being**＋
V-p.p.(Being accompanied) 形式：

Step 4 ➡ **be**動詞改成**Ving**，可以省略，就會變成：

改造後

~~Because~~	~~I~~	(Being) Accompanied by the bodyguards,
連接詞	主詞	動詞

I	felt very secure.
主詞	動詞

（有保鏢陪同，讓我感到非常放心。）

文法練習站 ❷

將下列句子以分詞構句改寫：

1. Because Jack was hit by a car, he was seriously injured.

   _____

   _____

2. Because the boy was abused by his parents, he was arranged to stay with a foster family.

   _____

   _____

3. If you are laid off, you can apply for unemployment benefits.

   _____

   _____

4. Because she was cheated by her husband, she decided to end her marriage.

   _____

   _____

5. Because the girl was bullied, she refused to go to school.

   _____

   _____

ANSWER

1. Hit by a car, Jack was seriously injured.
2. Abused by his parents, the boy was arranged to stay with a foster family.
3. Being laid off, you can apply for unemployment benefits.
4. Cheated by her husband, she decided to end her marriage.
5. Being bullied, the girl refused to go to school.

3 否定句

例1 改造前

Because	I	didn't	know where to go,
連接詞	主詞	否定詞	動詞

I	wandered toward the park.
主詞	動詞

把副詞子句簡化為分詞片語
分詞構句大變身→

Step 1 ➡ 確認前後兩個子句為同一人
（都是 I ）、去掉前半子句的主詞。

Step 2 ➡ 去掉連接詞 Because，

Step 3 ➡ 本句為主動語態→動詞變成 Ving 形式 (knowing)

Step 4 ➡ 去掉助動詞、保留否定詞 Not，就會變成：

改造後

~~Because~~	~~I~~	Not	knowing where to go,
~~連接詞~~	~~主詞~~	否定詞	動詞

I	wandered toward the park.
主詞	動詞

（因為不知道何去何從，我就漫步到公園。）

例2 改造前

If	a person	doesn't	feel loved,
連接詞	主詞	否定詞	動詞

he	will not have the ability to love.
主詞	動詞

把副詞子句簡化為分詞片語
分詞構句大變身→

Step 1 ⟹ 確認前後兩個子句為同一人
（都是**he**）、去掉前半子句的主詞。

Step 2 ⟹ 去掉連接詞**Because**，

Step 3 ⟹ 本句為主動語態→動詞變成**Ving**形式**(feeling)**

Step 4 ⟹ 去掉助動詞、保留否定詞**Not**，就會變成：

改造後

~~If~~	~~a person~~	Not	feeling loved,
連接詞	主詞	否定詞	動詞

a person	will not have the ability to love.
主詞	動詞

（不覺得被愛，一個人就不會有愛人的能力。）

文法練習站 ❸

將下列句子以分詞構句改寫

1. Because she doesn't have any friends here, she feels very lonely.

   _____

   _____

2. Because we don't love each other anymore, we decide to end
   our relationship.

   _____

   _____

3. If you don't follow the instructions, you will not have the software installed correctly.

_____

_____

4. Because I didn't know how to make beef noodles, I called my mother for help.

_____

_____

5. Because she has never seen the man before, she refused to let him in.

_____

_____

ANSWER

1. Not having any friends here, she feels very lonely.
2. Not loving each other anymore, we decide to end our relationship.
3. Not following the instructions, you will not have the software installed correctly.
4. Not knowing how to make beef noodles, I called my mother for help.
5. Never seen the man before, she refused to let him in.

例1 改造前

Because	we	have	bought the tickets,
連接詞	主詞	助動詞	動詞

we	will go to the concert anyways.
主詞	動詞

把副詞子句簡化為分詞片語
分詞構句大變身→

Step 1 → 確認前後兩個子句主詞相同
（都是 we）、去掉前半子句的主詞。

Step 2 → 去掉連接詞 Because，

Step 3 → 本句為完成式→助動詞變成 Ving 形式(Having)，
保留過去分詞，就會變成：

改造後

~~Because~~	~~we~~	Having	bought the tickets,
~~連接詞~~	~~主詞~~	助動詞	動詞

we	will go to the concert anyways.
主詞	動詞

（因為已經買票了，我們無論如何都會去音樂會。）

例2 改造前

Because	he	has	been here many times,
連接詞	主詞	助動詞	動詞

he	is not likely to get lost.
主詞	動詞

Step 1 ➡ 確認前後兩個子句主詞相同
（都是**he**）、去掉前半子句的主詞。

Step 2 ➡ 去掉連接詞**Because**，

Step 3 ➡ 本句為完成式→助動詞變成**Ving**形式**(Having)**，
保留過去分詞，就會變成：

把副詞子句簡化為分詞片語
分詞構句大變身

改造後

~~Because~~	~~he~~	Having	been here many times,
~~連接詞~~	~~主詞~~	助動詞	動詞

he	is not likely to get lost.
主詞	動詞

（來過這裡這麼多次，他不太可能會迷路的。）

文法練習站 ❹

以分詞構句改寫下列句子

1. Because I have saved enough money, I finally can go on a vacation.

   _____

   _____

2. We have known this man for many years, so we trust him.

   _____

   _____

3. Because he hasn't finished his assignment, he is not allowed to go with us.

   _____

   _____

4. Because she has lived in the USA since five, she can speak English like a native speaker.

_____

_____

5. Because we had been practicing very hard, we were not surprised about our winning.

_____

_____

5 被動完成式

例1 改造前

Because	the dog	has	been abandoned,
連接詞	主詞	助動詞	動詞

he	doesn't trust humans any more.
主詞	動詞

把副詞子句簡化為分詞片語
分詞構句大變身→

Step 1 ➞ 確認前後兩個子句主詞相同

（都是 **the dog**）、去掉前半子句的主詞。

Step 2 ➞ 去掉連接詞 **Because**，

Step 3 ➡ 本句為完成式→助動詞變成**Ving**形式**(Having)**，
保留 **been**＋過去分詞，就會變成：

改造後

~~Because~~	~~the dog~~	Having	been abandoned,
連接詞	主詞	助動詞	動詞

the dog	doesn't trust humans any more.
主詞	動詞

（因為曾經被拋棄，狗狗現在已經不再信任人。）

例2 改造前

Because	the man	had	been abused by his parents,
連接詞	主詞	助動詞	動詞

he	has developed a tendency towards violence.
主詞	動詞

分詞構句大變身→
把副詞子句簡化為分詞片語

Step 1 ➡ 確認前後兩個子句主詞相同
（都是 **the man**）、去掉前半子句的主詞。

Step 2 ➡ 去掉連接詞 **Because**，

Step 3 ➡ 本句為完成式→助動詞變成**Ving**形式**(Having)**，
保留 **been**＋過去分詞，就會變成：

改造後

~~Because~~	~~the man~~	Having	been abused by his parents,
連接詞	主詞	助動詞	動詞

the man	has developed a tendency towards violence.
主詞	動詞

（由於曾經被父母施暴，男子養成了暴力傾向。）

將下列句子以分詞構句改寫

1. Darren has been deceived by his best friend, so now he finds himself unable to believe anyone.

    _____

    _____

2. Because I have been treated unfairly, I have zero tolerance of injustice.

    _____

    _____

3. Because we have been warned several times, we avoid going out when it's dark outside.

    _____

    _____

4. Because they have been robbed on the streets, they are very cautious of strangers now.

    _____

    _____

5. Because she has been harassed at work, she never stays in the office alone. _____

    _____

ANSWER

1. Having been deceived by his best friend, now Darren finds himself unable to believe anyone.
2. Having been treated unfairly, I have zero tolerance of injustice.
3. Having been warned several times, we avoid going out when it's dark.
4. Having been robbed on the streets, they are very cautious of strangers now.
5. Having been harassed at work, she never stays in the office alone.

6 不省略連接詞的分詞構句

表時間的once/until，表條件的unless以及表對比或讓步的though等連接詞，通常帶有強調意味因而不予省略。

例1 改造前

Once	I	am available,	I	will call you back.
連接詞	主詞	動詞	主詞	動詞

把副詞子句簡化為分詞片語 →
分詞構句大變身→

Step 1 ➡ 確認前後兩個子句主詞相同
（都是 I ）、去掉前半子句的主詞。

Step 2 ➡ 表強調時間的分詞片語，連接詞 once 不省略。

Step 3 ➡ be 動詞改為 being，亦可同時省略，就會變成：

改造後

Once	~~I~~	(being) available,	I	will call you back.
連接詞	主詞	動詞	主詞	動詞

（一旦我有空，我就會回你電話。）

例2 改造前

Unless	we	have your support,	we	will not succeed.
連接詞	主詞	動詞	主詞	動詞

Step 1 ➡ 確認前後兩個子句主詞相同
（都是 we ）、去掉前半子句的主詞。

Step 2 ➡ 表條件的分詞片語，連接詞 unless 不省略。

Step 3 ➡ 動詞 have 改為 having，就會變成：

改造後

Unless	~~we~~	**having** your support,	we	will not succeed.
連接詞	主詞	動詞	主詞	動詞

（除非有你們的支持，否則我們不會成功。）

例3 改造前

Though	Steven	grew up in a broken home,	he	never abandoned himself.
連接詞	主詞	動詞	主詞	動詞

Step 1 ➡ 確認前後兩個子句主詞相同

（都是**we**）、去掉前半子句的主詞。

把副詞子句簡化為分詞片語 分詞構句大變身→

Step 2 ➡ 表讓步的分詞片語，連接詞**though**不省略。

Step 3 ➡ 動詞**grew**改為**growing**，就會變成：

改造後

Though	~~Steven~~	**growing** up in a broken home,	he	never abandoned himself.
連接詞	主詞	動詞	主詞	動詞

（雖然在一個破碎的家庭長大，Steven從來不自暴自棄。）

文法練習站 ❻

將下列句子以分詞構句改寫

1. Though he lost his limbs, he never gives up on life.

_____

_____

2. Once you're addicted to drugs, you have lost control of your life.

_____

_____

3. Though I have enough money, I'm not planning to buy a house of my own.

_____

_____

4. Once I finish the work, I'll go home for dinner.

_____

_____

5. Unless you see it with your own eyes, don't believe the rumor you hear.

_____

_____

ANSWER

1. Though losing his limbs, he never gives up on life.
2. Once (being) addicted to drugs, you have lost control of your life.
3. Though having enough money, I'm not planning to buy a house of my own.
4. Once finishing the work, I'll go home for dinner.
5. Unless seeing it with your own eyes, don't believe the rumor you hear.

獨立分詞構句

1 不省略主詞

當兩個句子的主詞不相同時，主詞不一定可以省略。當兩個主詞明確不同時，主詞不可省略。

例1 改造前

Because	it	was stormy,	our flight	was cancelled.
連接詞	主詞	動詞	主詞	動詞

把副詞子句簡化為分詞片語
分詞構句大變身→

Step 1 ➡ 去掉連接詞 because。

Step 2 ➡ 前後主詞不相同（it→天氣；our flight→班機），主詞不可省略。

Step 3 ➡ 主動語態，be動詞改為 being，就會變成：

改造後

~~Because~~	It	being stormy,	our flight	was cancelled.
連接詞	主詞	動詞	主詞	動詞

（我們的班機因暴風雨取消了。）

例2 改造前

If	time	permits,	I	will stop by your office and say hello.
連接詞	主詞	動詞	主詞	動詞

把副詞子句簡化為分詞片語
分詞構句大變身→

Step 1 ➡ 去掉連接詞 if。

Step 2 ➡ 前後主詞不相同（time→時間；I→我），主詞不可省略。

Step 3 ➡ 主動語態，動詞 permit 改為現在分詞 permitting，就會變成：

改造後

If	Time	permitting,	I	will stop by your office and say hello.
連接詞	主詞	動詞	主詞	動詞

（時間允許的話，我會順道經過你的公司跟你打個招呼。）

例3 改造前

When	Jane	was bullied at school,	Nina	Nina stood up for her.
連接詞	主詞	動詞	主詞	動詞

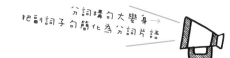

把副詞子句簡化為分詞片語 分詞構句大變身

Step 1 ➟ 去掉連接詞when。

Step 2 ➟ 前後主詞不相同（前半句是Jane；後半部是Nina），主詞不可省略。

Step 3 ➟ 被動語態，be動詞改為being，保留過去分詞，就會變成：

改造後

When	Jane	being bullied at school,	Nina	Nina stood up for her.
連接詞	主詞	動詞	主詞	動詞

（Jane在學校被霸凌時，Nina為她挺身而出。）

文法練習站 ❼

以分詞構句改寫下列句子

1. Because there was no electricity, we had to light up the candles.

_____

_____

2. If weather permits, we can go to the beach.

_____

_____

3. When his ex-girlfriend got married, he felt heartbroken.

_____

_____

4. Once the news was reported, everyone was anxious about the safety of their children.

_____

_____

5. Though her husband makes a lot of money, she lives a very simple life.

_____

_____

ANSWER

1. There being no electricity, we had to light up the candles.
2. Weather permitting, we can go to the beach.
3. His ex-girlfriend getting married, he felt heartbroken.
4. Once the news being reported, everyone was anxious about the safety of their children.
5. Though her husband making a lot of money, she lives a very simple life

2 可省略主詞

當副詞子句的主詞為「不特定的人」時，分詞片語的主詞就可以省略。

例1

Speaking of lunch,	I	really want to have spaghetti today.
動詞	主詞	動詞

原句為：

Since someone spoke of lunch, I really want to have spaghetti today.

（說到午餐，我今天真的很想吃義大利麵。）

例2

Judging from the woman's facial expression,	she	was definitely lying.
動詞	主詞	動詞

原句為：

原句為「從……來判斷」，不特定是由誰來判斷，可能是「我」也可能是「我們」，因此可以省略主詞，並將動詞judge改為現在分詞」。

When we judge from the woman's facial expression, (we can know that) she was definitely lying.

（從那女人的表情來判斷，她肯定在說謊。）

213

可省略主詞的獨立分詞片語有副詞功能，因此通常放在前面，修飾後面的句子，常用的獨立分詞片語：

- Considering... 若考慮……的話
- Judging from... 從……判斷
- Speaking of... 說到……
- Talking of ... 談到……
- Frankly speaking 坦白說
- Honestly speaking 老實說
- Generally speaking 一般說來……
- Strictly speaking 嚴格說起來……

例1

Considering **your** father's age,	a heart surgery	may not be a feasible treatment.
動詞	主詞	動詞

（考慮到你父親的年紀，心臟手術可能不是可行的治療方式。）

原句可能為：

考慮到」，不特定是由誰考慮，因此可以省略主詞，並將動詞 consider 改為現在分詞」。

If we consider your father's age, (we know that) a heart surgery may not be a feasible treatment.

例2

Talking **of French cuisine,**	I	have a very good recipe for beef bourguignon.
動詞	主詞	動詞

（說到法式料理，我有一份很棒的紅酒燉牛肉的食譜。）

原句可能為：

原句為「說到」，不特定是由誰在說，因此可以省略主詞，並將動詞talking改為現在分詞」。

When you talk of French cuisine, (you may want to know that) I have a very good recipe for beef bourguignon.

文法練習站 8

將提示做適當變化填入空格中，完成下列句子

1. _____ (speak) of paints, my bedroom needs painting.

2. _____ (consider) our finance condition, we shouldn't buy a new house now.

3. _____ (judge) from his income, there is no way that he could afford the car.

4. Generally _____ (speak), females are better language learners than males.

5. _____ (talk) of pets, I'm thinking about adopting a dog from the shelter.

ANSWER

1. Speaking	3. Judging	5. Taking
2. Considering	4. speaking	

Tips

★ 分詞片語除了用在分詞構句之外，也可以用在簡化句子中的形容詞子句。

【限定修飾的形容詞子句】

當句子中的連接詞（即關係代名詞）為主詞（如 who/which/that）時，可以簡化為分詞片語來修飾主詞。

簡化步驟與簡化副詞片語類同：

→步驟 1：去掉主詞
→步驟 2：判斷形容詞子句的語態為主動還是被動
　　　　主動語態：動詞改為現在分詞 V-ing
　　　　被動語態：動詞改為過去分詞 V-p.p.

★ 子句中有be動詞時，可以跟主詞一起省略。（不可只省略其一）。

【主動句】

例　改造前

My father is	the man	who is standing next to Mr. Lee.
主要子句	先行詞	形容詞子句

分詞構句大變身
→把形容詞子句
簡化為分詞片語

Step 1 ➡ 去掉形容詞子句的主詞（關係代名詞）
Step 2 ➡ 保留現在分詞 **standing**，
Step 3 ➡ be動詞跟主詞一起省略，就會變成：

改造後

My father is	the man	**standing next to Mr. Lee.**
主要子句	先行詞	形容詞子句簡化為分詞片語

（我父親就是站在李先生旁邊的那個男子。）

【被動句】

例1 改造前

The watch	which was stolen yesterday	was a gift from my grandfather.
先行詞	形容詞子句	主要子句

Step 1 ➡ 去掉關係子句的主詞（關係代名詞）

Step 2 ➡ 保留現在分詞 stolen，

Step 3 ➡ be 動詞跟主詞一起省略，就會變成：

> 分詞構句大變身
> →把形容詞子句
> 簡化為分詞片語

改造後

The watch	stolen yesterday	was a gift from my grandfather.
先行詞	形容詞子句	主要子句

（昨天被偷的那隻錶，是我爺爺送的禮物。）

例2 改造前

It is	a secret	which is known to only my very close friends.
主要子句	先行詞	形容詞子句

Step 1 ➡ 去掉關係子句的主詞（關係代名詞）

Step 2 ➡ 保留現在分詞 known，

Step 3 ➡ be 動詞跟主詞一起省略，就會變成：

> 分詞構句大變身
> →把形容詞子句
> 簡化為分詞片語

改造後

It is	a secret	known to only my very close friends.
主要子句	先行詞	形容詞子句

（這是一個只有我非常要好的朋友才知道的秘密。）

文法練習站 **5**

簡化形容詞子句，完成下列句子

1. The boy who is playing on the slide is my little brother.

   _____

   _____

2. Those who are spreading rumors in the office should all be fired.

   _____

   _____

3. The couple who was killed in the accident have three young children.

   _____

   _____

4. The bridge which was destroyed by the landslide was the only access to the village.

   _____

   _____

5. The novel which was written in English has been translated into 20 languages.

   _____

   _____

ANSWER

1. The boy playing on the slide is my little brother.
2. Those spreading rumors in the office should all be fired.
3. The couple killed in the accident have three young children.
4. The bridge destroyed by the landslide was the only access to the village.
5. The novel written in English has been translated into 20 languages.

Lesson 1
Lesson 2
Lesson 3
Lesson 4
Lesson 5
Lesson 6
Lesson 7
Lesson 8
Lesson 9
Lesson 10

Lesson 8

文法總複習

A 選擇

1. ( ) _____ the goal, we all felt excited.
   A. Achieved
   B. Have achieved
   C. Having achieved
   D. To achieve

2. ( ) _____ from Jane for years, I really miss her.
   A. Not having heard
   B. Haven't heard
   C. Having heard not
   D. No heard

3. ( ) _____ the case, we'd better hurry up.
   A. Being
   B. This being
   C. It be
   D. It has been

4. ( ) _____, the meeting will now be held at 2 p.m. tomorrow.
   A. To reschedule
   B. Rescheduling
   C. Having rescheduled
   D. Having been rescheduled

5. ( ) _____ an umbrella with him, Jack didn't get wet.
   A. Bring
   B. Brought
   C. Bringing
   D. Being brought

6. ( ) _____ for the best actor, Tommy Johnson was very excited and thankful.
   A. Nominated
   B. Having nominated
   C. Nominating
   D. Been nominated

7. ( ) _____ too much food, I am too full to move.
   A. Had
   B. Having
   B. Have eaten
   D. Have had

B 根據句意完成正確的分詞構句

1. _____ (If you turn) to the right, you'll see the bookstore next to the post office.

2. _____ (Because she doesn't have) a car, she commutes to work by train every day.

3. _____ (If you have done) your homework, you are allowed to watch TV.

4. The woman sat on the street, _____ (and she begged) people for money.

5. George looked at his wife, _____ (but he didn't say) anything.

6. _____ (Once you pass) the driving test, you will get a driver's license.

7. _____ (When you speak) of homework, I haven't done mine.

8. _____ (After electricity was discovered) by Benjamin Franklin, electricity has become the most important energy on Earth.

ANSWER

A. 選擇

1. C 2. A 3. B 4. D 5. C 6. A 7. B

B. 根據句意完成正確的分詞構句

1. Turning
2. Not having
3. Having done

4. begging
5. not saying
6. Once passing

7. Speaking
8. Discovered

Lesson 9

轉承語

Lesson 9

> 「然而，卻得不到結果。」
> However,
> I can't see our future.

轉承語

　　轉承詞是用來作為前後句子之間，語氣轉換或流暢連接的轉折詞。轉承詞可以是副詞、連接詞或片語，目的在於提供聽者或讀者有關下一句的性質或立場。

　　轉承詞的功能在於連接句子與段落之間的起承轉合，兩個句子之間應該使用什麼轉承詞，需根據前後句子之間的邏輯關係來做決定。寫作或演說時使用適當的轉承詞，除了可以讓語氣產生連貫性而顯得更為流暢之外，也可以讓聽者或讀者根據轉承詞的性質更快抓到重點。

　　本篇章將列舉各種性質與目的的常用轉承詞。熟悉並正確使用各種轉承詞，對英文寫作或演說絕對有一定的加分效果喔！

表達立場或意見

基本上、原則上	basically, in principle , principally
一般說來，大體而言	generally (speaking), in general, by and large, all in all, on the whole, overall
我認為	as far as I'm concerned, so far as I'm concerned, in my opinion, in my point of view, in my view, from what I can see, as I see it

例1

| Basically, | English is only a means of communication to me. |

（基本上，英文對我來說僅僅是一個溝通工具而已。）

例2

| Generally speaking, | girls are better at language than boys. |

（一般說來，女孩子比男孩子擅長語言。）

例3

| From what I can see, | Michael is a real asset to our company. |

（就我看來，Michael對我們公司來說是個真正的資產。）

表達立場或意見的轉承詞，通常放在句首喔！

文法練習站 ①

翻譯下列句子

1. 大體而言，你的計劃是可行得通的。(practicable)

_____

_____

2. 照我看來，這個案子很值得投資。(worth investing)

_____

_____

3. 原則上，只有二十歲及以上的公民有投票資格。(eligible to vote)

_____

_____

4. 一般而言，他在學校的表現相當好。

_____

_____

5. 我認為暑假的理想長度是一個半月。

_____

_____

ANSWER

1. By and large, your plan is practicable.
2. In my view, this project is worth investing.
3. In principle, only citizens who are 20 years old or above are eligible to vote.
4. Generally, his performance at school is quite good.
5. As far as I'm concerned, the ideal length of summer vacation is one and a half months.

 逐點列述

寫文章時，列點呈現超好用！

| 首先 | first of all, firstly, to begin with |

其次	secondly, in the second place
再者	also, furthermore, moreover, still
或者	alternatively
此外	in addition, additionally, besides, on top of, apart from, aside from, above and beyond
最後	finally, lastly, last but not least

例1 文章起頭、開門見山！

| **First of all,** | I would like to clarify my stance on this issue. |

（首先，我想要澄清我對這個問題的立場。）

例2 文章中間、延伸說明！

| The kitchen faucet is leaking. | **Besides,** | the toilet is clogged. |

（廚房水龍頭在漏水。此外，廁所馬桶也塞住了。）

例3 文章結尾、加強注意！

| **Last but not least,** | everyone has to be at school on time. |

（最後但並非最不重要的一點是，每個人都必須準時到校。）

225

文法練習站 ❷

翻譯下列句子

1. 我並沒有對我妻子不忠，而且，我們也沒有要離婚。

   _____

   _____

2. 首先，我想要謝謝你們來參加這個派對。

   _____

   _____

3. 游泳是很好的運動。再者，游泳的時候不會流汗。

   _____

   _____

4. 這個飯店離車站很近。此外，它還提供免費的早餐。

   _____

   _____

5. 最後但並非最不重要的是，永遠要注意你的個人物品。(keep an eye on)

   _____

   _____

ANSWER

1. I'm not cheating on my wife; also, we're not getting a divorce.
2. First of all, I would like to thank you for coming to this party.
3. Swimming is a very good exercise. Moreover, you don't sweat when swimming.
4. This hotel is close to the train station. In addition, it provides free breakfast.
5. Last but not least, always keep an eye on your personal belongings.

提出例證

寫作文時，舉例說明必備詞！

例如（放句首）	for example, for instance, take ... for example
諸如……（放句中）	such as, like
等等（放句尾）	and so on, and the like, etc.
根據……	according to ..., on the basis of ... , based on ..., as said by ... , in accordance with ...

呼應前面的「有不少疑點」

例1

| There are quite a few suspicious points in his testimony. | **For example,** | how did he know the door was unlocked? |

（他的證詞中有不少疑點。例如，他是怎麼知道門沒有鎖？）

呼應前面的「很多動物」

例2

| Many animals can make the perfect pets, | **such as** | dogs, cats and guinea pigs. |

（很多動物可以是完美的寵物，像是狗、貓和天竺鼠。）

為後半子句內容鋪成陳。

例3

| **According to** | the survey, over 30 percent of primary school students in this country are overweight. |

（根據調查，這個國家有超過百分之三十的小學生都體重過重。）

Tips ——————————————————————— 重點筆記

片語轉承詞中動詞或介系詞的受詞，必須
為「動名詞」或「名詞」。

例1

| According to | **the report,** | the man was murdered. |

（根據報導，男子是被殺害的。）

例2

| Take | **swimming** | for example, warm-up stretches can prevent muscle cramps for swimmers. |

（以游泳為例，暖身伸展可以為泳者預防肌肉抽筋。）

文法練習站 ❸ —————————————————————

填入適當的轉承詞

| for example | and so on | such as |
| based on | according to | |

1. Many jobs require good English proficiency, ＿＿＿＿＿＿ flight attendants and tour guides.

2. ＿＿＿＿＿＿ all the evidence presented at the trial, the man was sentenced ten years in prison.

3. I like all kinds of curry cuisines: Indian curry, Thai curry, Japanese curry_____.

4. There are so many unreasonable regulations of this school. _____, students are not allowed to bring cellphones to school.

5. _____the weather forecast, the typhoon will hit the island within 6 hours.

ANSWER

1. such as
2. Based on
3. and so on
4. For example
5. According to

表達時間順序

敘述故事時,事件順序、孰先孰後,清楚明瞭!

起初	at first, in the beginning, initially
不久之後	soon, before long, shortly, by and by, after a while, shortly afterwards
之後	afterwards, later on
與此同時,此時	meanwhile, in the meantime, at the same time, at this time
從那時起	from then on, ever since
從現在起	from now on
那時候,當時	then, at that time

229

例1

寫在故事開頭～

| At first, | I didn't know that he was hatching conspiracy against the government. |

（一開始，我並不知道他正在策劃反抗政府的陰謀活動。）

例2

前後兩件事同時進行～

| They were busy planning for their wedding. | In the meantime, | they were thinking to buy a house. |

（他們正忙著準備他們的婚禮。同時，他們也打算買房子。）

例3

時間點從當下往後延伸～

| From now on, | I will never ask you for help. |

（從現在起，我將不會再找你幫忙。）

文法練習站 ❹

選出適當轉承詞填入空格中，以完成此篇故事

| from then on | shortly afterwards | later on |
| in the meantime | in the beginning | |

Mr. and Mrs. Lin moved into a dream house in the suburbs. (1)_____, everything was perfect. (2) _____, strange things started happening in the house. For example, they always had unexpected power failures. One day, they found a dead mouse in the kitchen sink. (3) _____, Mrs. Lin never stepped into the kitchen again. (4) _____, Mr. Lin was diagnosed with some weird disease. They decided to move out of the house, and (5) _____, Mr. Lin was fully recovered and everything went back to normal.

ANSWER

1. In the beginning
2. Later on
3. From then on
4. In the meantime
5. shortly afterwards

 # 開啟話題或轉換話題

為了避免太跳tone，你需要這類的轉承詞！

關於……	with regard to ... , with respect to ... , regarding..., in reference to ... , in relation to ...
提到……	when it comes to ... , speaking of ...
至於……	as for ... , as to ...
順帶一提	by the way

例1

突然想到你的請求！

With regard to your request, we will send a helper to assist you.

（關於您的請求，我們將派一名幫手去協助您。）

例2

突然提到奧客這件事……

| When it comes to | dealing with difficult customers, Jenny is an expert. |

（講到應付奧客，Jenny是個專家。）

例3

不經意地帶出真正想講的話題……

| By the way, | do you have any plans for tonight? |

（對了，你今天晚上有任何計劃嗎？）

文法練習站 ❺

選出適當的轉承詞填入空格中，以完成句子

| with regard to | when it comes to | by the way |
| as for | speaking of | |

1. _____ tennis, my brother is really good at it.

2. _____ your inquiry, underwear is not returnable because of potential hygiene reason.

3. _____, what are you going to do after school?

4. It is reported that the government will raise house tax next year. _____ which, it just occurred to me that I haven't paid my taxes yet.

5. _____ my work experience, I have three years' experience of working in the tourism industry.

ANSWER

1. When it comes to
2. With regard to
3. By the way
4. Speaking of
5. As for

加強語氣

文章前面有些鋪陳，要講到重點時，就要用到這些轉承詞！

當然地，無疑地	certainly, of course, undoubtedly, unquestionably
特別是，尤其，更重要的是	in particular, particularly, above all, especially, specifically, more importantly, what's more
最重要的是	most importantly, most important of all
最糟糕的是	the worst of all
更糟糕的是	what's worse
無論如何，反正，總之	anyway(s), in any case, anyhow, for better or worse
遑論，更不用說	needless to say

un-question-abl-y 表示「無法去質疑這件事情」！

例1

Unquestionably,	Emma is the strongest candidate for the job.

（毫無疑問地，Emma是這份工作所有應徵者中條件最強的。）

例2

講到這邊，重點來囉！

To lose weight healthily, you must eat healthy.	**Most important of all,**	you should exercise regularly.

（要健康地減重，你一定要吃得健康。最重要的是，你應該要規律地運動。）

例3

沒有例外、不能找藉口喔！

In any case,	you must settle the payment by the end of the month.

（無論如何，你一定得在這個月底之前把款項繳清。）

文法練習站 ❻

選出適當的轉承詞填入空格中，以完成句子

most importantly	in particular	for better or worse
what's more	needless to say	

1. John didn't hand in his homework again. _____, he was punished by the teacher.

2. To protect yourself from the sun, you must wear sunglasses. _____, apply sunscreen before going outdoors.

3. I quite enjoyed the concert; _____, I loved the solo.

4. _____, he is my father, and he needs me now.

5. Peter fell off the tree; _____, he broke his arm.

ANSWER

1. Needless to say
2. Most importantly
3. in particular
4. For better or worse
5. what's more

 表達對比

陳述不同觀點：	on the one hand, ..., on the other hand, ...
一方面……，	for one thing, ..., for another, ...
另一方面則……	in one respect, in another
一樣地，相同地	likewise, similarly, in common with ...
一如往常地	as usual
相反地	on the contrary, the other way round, conversely, contrary to ..., instead,
與……相較	in comparison with ...
相對於……	in contrast with ..., in contrast to ..., by contrast

例1

我們是好朋友喔！

On the one hand,	I'd like to start a family with Lily, but	on the other hand,

I quite enjoy the life I'm living at the moment.

（一方面，我想跟Lily一起共組家庭，但是另一方面，我相當享受我目前的生活。）

例2

| Mary's work attitude is not very good; | likewise, | her work performance is unsatisfactory. |

（Mary的工作態度不是非常好；同樣的，她的工作表現也差強人意。）

例3

| He didn't buy the computer. | Instead, | he bought a smartphone. |

（他沒有買電腦，卻反而買了一支智慧型手機。）

文法練習站 ❼

選出適當的轉承詞填入空格中，以完成句子

in comparison with   for one thing, for another   instead
on the contrary   as usual

1. We shouldn't buy the car. _____, we don't need it; _____, we can't afford it.

2. _____ his brother, Jack is more careful and thoughtful.

3. Dad got up very early this morning, and _____, he went jogging before breakfast.

4. He didn't ask his wife for help; _____, he asked his mother.

5. I thought the party was going to be a disaster, but _____, it turned out to be very successful.

ANSWER

1. For one thing ; for another	4. instead/on the contrary
2. In comparison with	5. on the contrary/instead
3. as usual	

表示轉折或讓步

然而	however, nevertheless, nonetheless
即使，不管	in spite of, despite, regardless of, even though, although
雖然，儘管	although, while

例1

怎麼會不接受呢!?

nevertheless要放在句首或者分號之後喔！

She knew it was a great job offer;	**nevertheless,**	she didn't accept it.

（她知道那是個很棒的工作機會，但是她並沒有接受。）

例2

真沒想到她這麼堅強！

Despite後面要接名詞喔！

Despite	adverse circumstances, she raised her three children on her own.

（儘管處在惡劣的環境中，她仍然靠自己養大三個孩子。）

例3

我們追求的東西不一樣！

While後面要接子句喔！

While | most people spend their lifetime pursuing fame and wealth, we value health and happiness beyond all things.

（儘管大部份的人終其一生都在追求名利，我們把健康與幸福看得比什麼都重要。）

文法練習站 ❽

圈出正確的轉承詞，以完成句子

1. The task was a real challenge; (nevertheless, although) he didn't fall back.

2. (While, In spite of) I like the car, I'm not happy with the price.

3. (Even though, Despite) the vile weather, the concert took place as scheduled.

4. The test was difficult; (regardless of, however), he passed it.

5. (Although, Nevertheless) the dress was not fancy, it's my favorite one.

ANSWER

1.nevertheless	3.Despite	5.Although
2.While	4.however	

表示原因或結果

由於， 為了……之故	because of ..., due to ..., owing to ..., as a result of ..., thanks to ..., in consequence of ..., on account of ..., by reason of ..., in virtue of ...
有鑒於	in view of ..., seeing that ..., in consideration of ..., considering ...
因此，為此，結果	as a result, for this reason, consequently, as a consequence, on this account, therefore, hence, accordingly

 和 because of 一樣的用法

 例1

Owing to	the vile weather, we had no option but to close the airport.

（由於天氣惡劣，我們不得不關閉機場。）

owing to 也可以放在句中喔！如：We had no option but to close the airport **owing to** the vile weather.

 和 Considering 一樣的用法

 例2

In consideration of	his health condition, the doctor insisted that he should stay in the hospital.

（考慮到他的健康情況，醫生堅持他應該要住院。）

in consideration of 後面接名詞喔！

239

例3

和 therefore 一樣的用法

| His performance at work was outstanding. | Hence, | he deserved a raise and a promotion. |

（他的工作表現實在太優異了。
　因此，他值得獲得薪資加給與職務晉升。）

Hence要放在句首或者
分號後面使用喔！

文法練習站 ❾

圈出正確的轉承詞，以完成句子

1. We can't afford a new car. (Because of, Therefore), we bought a used one.

2. (Considering, Owing to) her age, she's done a very good job.

3. (In consideration of, Thanks to) your advice, I accomplished the mission with little effort.

4. It was the third time that Frank left early without cause. (On this account, In view of), he was fired.

5. The only access was blocked. (As a consequence, Seeing that), we couldn't enter the village.

ANSWER

1. Therefore
2. Considering
3. Thanks to

4. On this account
5. As a consequence

 **提出解釋或補充說明**

事實上，實際上	in fact, as a matter of fact, actually, in reality, in truth
換句話說，也就是說	in other words, that is (to say), to put it in another way, to put it differently,
既然那樣	in that case

例1

 補充說明

原來前面提到的是推測！確切原因是不明的！

In fact,	no one knows exactly how dinosaurs died out.

（事實上，沒有人確實知道恐龍是怎麼滅亡的。）

例2

原來 "between jobs" 在兩個工作中間，指的是待業中！

 換句話說

My brother is between jobs.	**That is,**	he is unemployed at the moment.

（我哥哥正在待業中。也就是説，他現在處在失業狀態。）

例3

 以這為前題⋯⋯⋯

知道你是素食者之後，就想趕快給你建議！

You're a vegetarian?	**In that case,**	why didn't you order a vegetarian meal?

（你是個素食者？既然那樣，你為何不點素食餐？）

圈出適當的轉承詞，以完成句子

1. You don't like living in the city? (In that case, In other words), why don't you move to the countryside?

2. You do not meet our requirements for the job. (That is to say, In fact), your application for the job was unsuccessful.

3. He told the teacher he left his homework at home, but (in that case, in fact), he didn't do it at all.

4. Her parents are out of town. (In reality, In other words), he's home alone now.

5. I don't like any meat. (As a matter of fact, in that case), I'm a vegetarian.

ANSWER

1. In that case
2. That is to say
3. in fact
4. In other words
5. As a matter of fact

表達結論

簡而言之	to put it in a nutshell, to put it briefly, in brief, in short, to put it simply, in a word
總之	in sum, to sum up, in summary, in conclusion, to conclude, all in all, altogether

用簡短的方式講

例1

In short可以摘要文章重點。

In short, money is the root of all evil.

（簡而言之，金錢就是萬惡之源。）

用簡短的方式講

例2

To sum up可以總結文章的論點。

To sum up, for a happy marriage you must learn to compromise with your significant other.

（總之，要有一個幸福的婚姻，你必須要學著向你的另一半妥協。）

 文法練習站 ⑪

翻譯下列句子

1. 簡單來說，你必須先愛自己才能愛其他人。

_____

2. 以一言以蔽之，學習永遠不嫌晚。

_____

3. 總而言之，家庭是最重要的。

_____

4. 簡短來說，我感謝所有曾經幫助過我的人。

_____

5. 結論就是，機會只留給準備好的人。

_____

ANSWER

1. In short, you have to love yourself before you can love someone else.
2. In a word, it's never too late to learn.
3. All in all, family matters most.
4. To put it briefly, I am thankful for all those who have helped me.
5. In conclusion, opportunities are only for the people who are prepared.

文法總複習

A▶ 選擇

1. (　) I have been to several Southeast Asian countries, _____ Nepal, Cambodia, Thailand and Malaysia.
   A. as for　　B. and so on　　C. such as　　D. for instance

2. (　) Anne has quite a few shortcomings. _____, she can't keep secrets.
   A. Considering　　　B. Thanks to
   C. Despite　　　　　D. For example

3. (　) ____ your encouragement, I never gave up pursuing my dream.
   A. Because of　　　B. Because
   C. As for　　　　　D. In spite of

4. (　) _____ the accommodation, please tell me the exact number of people who are going so I can book the hotel room in advance.
   A. According to　　　B. Considering
   C. With respect to　　D. To sum up

5. (　) _____ your efforts, our proposal has been adopted.
   A. as usual　　B. Owing to　　C. Similarly　　D. Instead

6. (　) I overslept myself and _____ was late for school.
   A. consequently　　　B. as a result of
   C. in addition　　　　D. while

7. (　) _____ English, Jane can also speak French and German.
   A. In addition to　　　B. Moreover
   C. What's more　　　　D. Furthermore

8. (　) _____, money can't buy everything.
   A. In virtue of　　　B. Later on
   C. Alternatively　　　D. In brief

9. ( ) _____ zodiac signs, Josephine can talk endlessly.
   A. Consequently   B. Considering
   C. Speaking of   D. In view of

10. ( )_____ most Chinese parents, my mother is rather open-minded.
    A. In consideration of   B. In contrast to
    C. In accordance with   D. in conclusion

B 配合題，填入適當的轉折詞代號

(A) To put it in another way	(B) For better or worse
(C) as a result	(D) Even though
(E) In one respect; in another	

1. _____ , Paul is a perfectionist; _____ , he is very fastidious.

2. She gave her son whatever he wanted; _____ , he was totally spoilt.

3. _____ he lost all his limbs, he never lost his will to live.

4. You are the owner of your life. _____ , no one has power over you unless you give it to them.

5. _____ , things will turn out fine.

ANSWER

A. 選擇

1. C   2. D   3. A   4. C   5. B   6. A   7. A   8. D   9. C   10. B

B. 配合題，填入適當的轉折詞代號

1. E ; E   2. C   3. D   4. A   5. B